The Glory Wind

Valerie Sherrard

Fitzhenry & Whiteside

Published in Canada by Fitzhenry & Whiteside
195 Allstate Parkway, Markham, Ontario L3R 4T8

Published in the United States by Fitzhenry & Whiteside,
311 Washington Street, Brighton, Massachusetts 02135

www.fitzhenry.ca   godwit@fitzhenry.ca

10 9 8 7 6 5 4 3 2

Library and Archives Canada Cataloguing in Publication
Sherrard, Valerie
      The glory wind / Valerie Sherrard.

ISBN 978-1-55455-170-5
      I. Title.

PS8587.H3867G56 2010   jC813'.6   C2010-904390-1

U.S. Publisher Cataloging-in-Publication Data (Library of Congress Standards)

Sherrard, Valerie.
   The glory wind / Valerie Sherrard.
[192] p. : cm.

Summary: Luke meets Gracie, and despite her being a girl, they become close friends. When
the citizens of the small, rural, 1940s town that Luke lives in learn that Gracie and her mother
have a shady past, Luke must decide whether he will stand up for his new friend or save his own
reputation.
ISBN-13: 978-1-55455-170-5 .

1. Interpersonal relations – Juvenile fiction. 2. Courage – Juvenile fiction. I. Title.
[Fic] dc22   PZ7.S5477Gl 2010

Fitzhenry & Whiteside acknowledges with thanks the Canada Council for the Arts, and the
Ontario Arts Council for their support of our publishing program. We acknowledge the finan-
cial support of the Government of Canada through the Book Publishing Industry Development
Program (BPIDP) for our publishing activities.

Canada Council   Conseil des Arts
for the Arts   du Canada

ONTARIO ARTS COUNCIL
CONSEIL DES ARTS DE L'ONTARIO

Cover and interior design by Erik Mohr
Cover illustration by Erik Mohr

Printed in Canada

Preserving our environment
Fitzhenry & Whiteside Ltd. chose to print the pages of this
book on recycled paper and saved these resources[1]:

energy	water	greenhouse gases	solid waste
16 million BTUs	68,293 L	1,815 kg	519 kg

Printed by **Webcom Inc.** on
Legacy Hi-Bulk Natural 100% post-consumer waste.

ANCIENT FOREST™
FRIENDLY

39 trees were saved
for our forests

[1]Estimates were made using the Environmental Defense Paper Calculator.

FSC
www.fsc.org
MIX
Paper from
responsible sources
FSC® C004071

You can always tell a real friend:
when you've made a fool of yourself he doesn't
feel you've done a permanent job.
- Laurence J. Peter

By this, and many other definitions,
I am blessed with more than my share of real friends.
This book is for:

Janet Aube
Darlene Cowton
Karen Gauvin
John Hambrook
Marsha Skrypuch

ACKNOWLEDGEMENTS

Many, many thanks to my fabulous editor, Christie Harkin. In addition to her brilliant editorial guidance, I am ever so grateful for her patience, her support and her friendship.

Love and thanks to my husband, Brent, who has been unwavering in his support of my work. His enthusiasm for this story in particular has meant more to me than he will ever know.

Some of the characters in *The Glory Wind* were named by and for students. For these contributions, sincere thanks go to Karly Grasse, Kevin Sarrazin, and Leah Zecchino.

PART ONE

The Arrival

We like to measure.

We like to know the size and strength and movement of a thing.

Measuring helps us understand where and how something fits into our world.

Tornados are measured on a scale called the Fujita scale (also known as the F-Scale) which is named for Dr. Tetsuya Theodore "Ted" Fujita. Dr. Fujita's research unlocked many of the mysteries of tornados.

The F-Scale measures a tornado's strength—from F0, the least intense, all the way up to F5, which is the most intense.

Chapter One

When I think about all the circumstances that *might* have been part of our first meeting, I can't help but be glad for the way it actually happened.

It was 1946 and a scorching July afternoon. I sometimes wish I knew the exact date, but maybe it's best that I don't. Maybe being whittled down to a single day would make it too narrow and small. Some events need more breathing room than others. This was one of them.

I was crossing through the field, coming back from Dempsey's farm. I'd gone there hoping to find Keane Dempsey at home and bored. That was a requirement for him to let me stick around.

"You might as well know," he liked to tell me, "that you wouldn't be here if I wasn't bored out of my skull." Then he'd tap his head. I was never exactly sure what the head tap meant, and it never seemed like a good idea to ask.

Keane said I was lucky he *ever* hung out with a little kid like me. At thirteen, he had a two-year advantage, plus he told me once he was growing hair in places I'd never guess. There was no sign of a beard starting, and I spent a lot of time wondering about the location of these mysterious hairs of his.

I never said anything back; he was the only kid around whose place was close enough for me to walk to. Most farms around Junction are on the north side of town, where the land is better for crops. Of the few farms here on the south side, the Dempseys' was the only other one with a kid near my age. He could be a pain sometimes, but having someone to do things with once in a while was better than nothing.

Besides, his uncle from North Dakota had sent him an old copy of Keds Handbook of Sports and Games last year. You can spend a whole afternoon doing some of the things in there. Keane liked the games best, but there were exercises too, and we always worked on them some. We figured that if we kept at it regular, we'd eventually have muscles like Charles Atlas, The World's Most Perfectly Developed Man.

But none of that mattered that day. Mrs. Dempsey gave me a cookie and the news that Keane had gone to Malcolm Nessling's place and wouldn't be back before supper chores.

I headed home, cutting through the field where our sheep grazed, and crossed a second field to a double row of lodgepole pines. Beyond that was a hilly area, rock-peppered with a scattered mix of trees and shrubs. I decided to stop there for a while.

It's my favourite place to be when I'm alone.

Except, I wasn't.

She was partly hidden by a bush, kneeling on the ground with her hands bunched in front of her chin as though she were praying. Her face was framed by brown hair that sprang from her head in loops and spirals. The position she was in put me in mind of an oversized prairie dog in spite of the navy skirt and red blouse she was wearing.

The sound of my feet scuffing along the ground must have reached her because all of a sudden her head popped up. She darted looks about until she saw me. Her hands dropped to her sides and she fixed her eyes on me. I had the odd sensation that *I* was trespassing.

I stood there immobile and confused as she stared at me. After all, there'd never been a little girl in my field before, least of all one in such an odd pose.

She moved first, getting to her feet, brushing her knees off, and crossing her arms over her chest. She maintained that pose for a moment or two, and then walked toward me. As she approached, she looked at me like I was a big, ugly toad that was almost certainly going to give her warts.

"Who are you?" she demanded.

"Luke."

"I'm *Gracie*." She made it sound like a grand declaration. "Is this *your* field, *Luke*?"

I wasn't entirely sure what she meant by the question. Obviously, the land couldn't belong to an eleven-year-old boy.

"Well, *is* it?"

I could see that she meant to keep right on asking until I came up with some kind of answer so I said yes, it was my field.

Gracie nodded. Then she said, "Well, I'm not leaving, if that's what you think."

I wanted to answer her, to say something that would let her know she wasn't going to prance onto my property and start acting like the boss, but my head felt kind of befuddled. After a few seconds, and doubtless emboldened by my silence, Gracie put her hands on her hips. I watched her in fascinated confusion, wondering what might come out of her next.

"*My* daddy was a war hero," she said.

It was the last thing I might have expected and yet I don't recall being particularly surprised.

"Is that so?" I said.

"Of course it is!" Her right hand left its hip long enough to wag a finger at me. "He died fighting for his country."

I agreed that would make him a hero. And I hoped she wouldn't ask about my father and what he'd been doing during the war.

Luckily, Gracie was busy with her own thoughts.

"He *doted* on me." She thrust her head forward and shook it. "See this? My daddy *loved* my curly hair."

I offered a sort of grunt in reply, so as not to be rude. It seemed to be enough for her, for she went on after a quick pause to shove the curly-hair-her-daddy-had-loved back away from her face.

"I'm eleven now!" she declared next. "I had my birthday in June. It was just a few weeks ago, on the 22nd. I got a cake with a balloon tied to it and a new pair of patent leather shoes. My mother bought them for me at Eaton's

Department Store in Winnipeg. It's the biggest, grandest store you ever did see."

"I've been there hundreds of times," I said. Actually, I'd been there twice.

"Do you have any snakes?"

The change of subject threw me. It would be a while before I'd get used to Gracie's ability to switch topics almost mid-sentence. Even so, I managed to ask what she meant.

"You mean do I have any snakes *on* me...or are there any on the property?"

"*On* you?" She rolled her eyes and laughed. Her hair shook and shimmered like a wild waterfall. "Why would you have snakes *on* you?"

I wished with all my might that I had a snake in my pocket or down my shirt. But, of course, I didn't.

"What do you want a snake for, anyway?" I asked.

"For a snake race." She glanced at me and seemed to decide that I needed a full explanation. "We'd need two of them."

"Well, who wouldn't know *that*?" I said. "Anyone knows you can't race a snake alone." The truth was I'd never raced snakes. The idea had never occurred to me.

But Gracie had already moved on. "I can do all my times tables right up to seven. Can you?"

Here, at least, I had her. "To nine," I said proudly, ready to prove it.

"Arithmetic is boring anyway," she said. She offered an exaggerated yawn and then clapped her hands so suddenly that I jumped back a little. "My mother is making raspberry jam! Do you want to come to my place and have a slice of bread and jam?"

Her place? It hadn't crossed my mind to wonder where she lived but as soon as she said the words I realized that it was probably the Sharpe place. It had been empty for a couple of years, ever since old widow Sharpe had died.

Alden Sharpe, her only son, was married to a girl from Winnipeg and he worked in the city as a shoe salesman. He liked to say that leaving Junction was the best move he ever made. After his mother's funeral he'd put the family home up for sale but times being what they were, there'd been no offers. We'd heard last month that he'd rented the place, except when weeks went by without a tenant it seemed that the rumour wasn't true.

"Where do you live?" I asked, just in case.

Gracie smiled. Her gold-flecked hazel eyes shone in the

light and her loose curls formed a shining halo around her small, sun-browned face. Something odd happened in my stomach.

"We moved into the house over there," she said with a wave in the right direction.

"When'd you do that?"

"Yesterday. So, do you want to come for bread 'n jam or not?"

The thought of fresh warm jam on a piece of bread had taken hold on me, so I didn't need any persuasion.

The house looked pretty much as it always had, which surprised me a little. I guess I'd expected something different, something that proved there were new people living inside. Instead, it stood there, as dark and unwelcoming as it had been when old widow Sharpe had lived there.

Gracie flung the door open and stomped in noisily, calling to her mother that she'd brought Luke over and was the jam ready and could we have some.

A head peeked out from the kitchen, broke into a smile, and told us to c'mon in and plunk ourselves down. I could smell the jam as we made our way to the kitchen, twisting in and around boxes and suitcases that were scattered about the floor.

"Well, good for you, Gracie!" her mother said, leaning down to kiss Gracie on the forehead. "You found yourself a friend right off. Hello, Luke! I'm Raedine."

She turned and reached out to me. I had a horrifying thought that she was going to kiss me too, but all she did was take my arm and tug me over to the table, which was covered with stacks of dishes and things. It seemed she'd begun the unpacking process but hadn't gotten very far with it.

"I just found some jars in the nick of time," she said, plopping down on a stool near the counter. "Didn't have time to put anything away while I looked. I suppose most folks would think it was crazy to be doing this before we've even unpacked. But doesn't it make the house smell heavenly?"

As she sawed slices from a loaf of bread and smeared them with the fresh confection, I tried to but couldn't picture my mother leaving a huge mess all over the house so she could go off to pick berries and make jam.

"You want a cup of tea with this, Luke?"

I said no thanks to the tea and was given a mug of cold water instead. Then she balanced a plate with my slice of bread on it on top of some cups and saucers in front of me. It was unbelievably delicious but I didn't tell her that in case she thought I was hinting for more. Even though the war was over, sugar still had to be used sparingly.

When we'd finished our bread, Gracie took me upstairs to see her room. A blanket had been tacked over the window and, like the rest of the house, there were things all over the place.

"I haven't decided what to call it yet," she told me, holding her arms wide apart and twirling.

"You're going to *name* your room?"

"Of course I am." She seemed puzzled that anyone would be surprised at that.

A little while later, as I made my way home, I thought about that, and about racing snakes, and about mothers who made jam while their house was upside-down messy.

And for some reason that wasn't clear to me, I said nothing to my folks about having met our new neighbours.

Chapter Two

There's no hurrying two stubborn people when they're at odds about something, which is why the waiting line at the post office had come to a standstill. Like a lot of arguments, it was hard to tell who started it.

It was the day after I'd met Gracie, and I was in town with my mother, already fidgeting and regretting my decision to come.

"You know perfectly well that I don't accept these." Mrs. Melchyn's voice sounded as if the postmaster, Ned Aukland, had offered her a handful of spittlebugs instead of the coins he was holding out.

"The tombac is legal tender in this country, ma'am." Ned set the change down in front of her and crossed his arms over his chest.

I listened while Mrs. Melchyn declared that she'd accept

the Victory Nickel when it actually contained nickel, and not one minute sooner. By then the argument had gone on for three or four minutes while the rest of us stood there waiting.

My attention drifted around the room, landing on a silvery web over the door. A fat spider hunched there, still as a stone, waiting and watching. Picturing the spider's lightning strike and the battle that would follow, I willed a fly that was buzzing against the windowpane to venture over. But minutes dragged along without a sign of lunch delivering itself to the spider.

I lost interest. My focus moved along, looking for a place to settle. The nickel argument was still going on and it seemed as though everything else in the room was frozen like it was in a photograph.

I tapped my mother's arm.

"Can I wait outside?"

"Well, all right, but stay on the step."

I was out the door like a shot. Ma has been known to change her mind and I wasn't taking any chances. I planted myself on the top step and looked around, just in case any of my friends were in town.

No such luck. I did see Mrs. Naismith, but I leaned

forward, folded my arms over my knees, and ducked my head in there before she noticed me. Mrs. Naismith is the grade five and six Sunday School teacher. Anytime I see her outside of church she asks me if I have my memory work done. Then she'll stand there and prompt me by reciting a few words at a time, like I might suddenly remember what comes next. She does that even if it's only Monday, though why she'd think anyone would know it on Monday, I have no idea.

I always do my Sunday School lesson on Saturday, right after my bath. Ma makes me say my memory verse for her on Sunday morning, to make sure I have it right. Then Pa gives me a penny for the collection plate. That makes me feel like I'm earning the money I give to God, though what good a penny is to Him I couldn't say. Sometimes I think I could make better use of those pennies on some jawbreakers at Clive's General Store, and that kind of sinful thought reminds me that I need to get to church all right.

I gave Mrs. Naismith lots of time to pass by before peeking out and then lifting my head. That's when I saw Gracie and her mother. They were just emerging from the Prairie Inn across the street.

The Glory Wind

Raedine had on lipstick the colour of an overripe tomato and a bright blue dress with wide shoulders. She looked like a movie star. Gracie was wearing a yellow dress with short sleeves and a skirt that puffed out near the bottom. A matching yellow ribbon did its best to control a clump of her unruly hair.

They'd crossed to my side of the street before Gracie saw me. The second she did, she began waving frantically, as though I might not have seen her there.

I gave a weak wave in return and wondered if it was too late to go back inside the post office. A feeling of panic had swept over me, which was odd, since I had no reason to avoid her.

Either way, it didn't matter because while I was thinking on it, Gracie was coming my way, her dress and hair bouncing as she hurried over.

"Luke!" she said. "You didn't tell me you were going to be in town today!"

Her tone of voice suggested that I should have reported my plans to her. All I said was, "Well, I am."

"I can *see* that," Gracie said. Laughter poured out of her in peals that sounded like a cluster of bells gone wild. And then, all of a sudden, she stepped forward and slugged me as hard as any guy my age could do. It threw my shoulder back, but only because I hadn't been expecting it.

"Hey!" I yelped, regretting it while it was still leaving my mouth. I sounded like a pup that'd gotten his paw stepped on.

"Now, Gracie, there's no need of that," Raedine said. "You're just too rough sometimes! You tell Luke you're sorry."

"That's okay," I said quickly. Gracie ignored me.

"I'm *awfully* sorry if I hurt you, Luke," she said. Her eyes were still laughing.

"You *didn't* hurt me!" I said. I could feel myself shrinking, right there in the middle of Junction. "I was just *surprised*, is all," I added, hoping that would explain my outburst to Gracie. And to anyone else who might be watching.

"Oh, then I'm *sorry* for *surprising* you, Luke," Gracie said.

Before I could even think of what to say to that, the door of the post office opened and Mrs. Melchyn emerged. She stopped to fix her hat before descending the stairs with her purse clutched against her. A glance at her face told me she'd won the argument about the tombac nickel.

As Mrs. Melchyn reached the bottom step, Gracie

turned to her. "How do, ma'am? My name is Gracie Moor and this is my mother Raedine Moor and we're new in town."

"Oh!" Mrs. Melchyn said. She smiled and nodded to Gracie and then shook Raedine's hand. She introduced herself and said they were very welcome in Junction. Then she asked where they were from and what Raedine's people did.

"I'm afraid I *have* no people," Raedine said. Her smile faltered and fell. I found myself staring at her mouth, sad and trembling, with that bright red lipstick decorating it.

"Now that's a shame," Mrs. Melchyn said. I think she was going to say something else but Ma came out of the post office just then.

"Well, aren't you just full of surprises," Ma said to me.

I had no idea what she meant.

"Aren't you going to introduce me to this young lady?" she asked. There was a strange smile on her face.

"That's Gracie," I said, pointing, "and her mom, Rae ... uh, Mrs. Moor."

Gracie smiled and said, "How do you do, ma'am?" in the most innocent voice you ever heard. You'd never have guessed she'd been slugging me on the arm a minute before.

"Pleased to meet you both," Ma said. "I'm Alice Haliwell, Luke's mother. Welcome to Junction."

"We met your boy Luke the other day," Raedine told her. "And thank you—we're glad to be here. It seems like a nice little town." She paused and took a deep breath, then blurted, "I hope I did the right thing, coming here. I just felt I had to get away from all the memories after my husband died."

"Oh, I'm so sorry!" My mother reached a hand out and touched Raedine's arm. "Are there just the two of you?"

"Yes. Gracie is the only child my husband and I were blessed with." She cleared her throat and her eyes strayed to the ground.

"My daddy *adored* my curly hair," Gracie said.

"I'm sure he did, honey. It's very pretty." Ma turned her attention back to Raedine. "Do you have family in these parts?"

"No, nobody," Raedine said. "I'm afraid it's just me and Gracie from here on in."

"Where are you living?"

"Why, right next door to you, if I understand correctly. We've rented a house from Mr. Alden Sharpe."

"Oh, yes. Then we're neighbours!" Ma said. "How nice!"

The Glory Wind

"Tell them about your job!" Gracie said, patting the back of her mother's hand.

Raedine hesitated ever so slightly before smiling and telling us that she'd managed to get a position at the Prairie Inn.

"The Prairie Inn," Ma echoed. "Well now." Even only half paying attention, I could see she wasn't impressed.

"Yes," Raedine said. "Wasn't I lucky to find something so quickly, what with jobs being so scarce and all?"

"Yes, of course." Ma smiled and nodded. "You and Gracie must come for dinner so we can get acquainted. Saturday, if you're free."

"Roasted chicken with bread stuffing is my favourite," Gracie declared.

Raedine told her it wasn't ladylike to plan the menu for your hostess, and Ma said that was just fine and she was quite sure roasted chicken was the very thing she'd had in mind anyway.

* * *

At dinner that night, Ma told Pa about meeting Raedine and Gracie.

"You say she's going to be working at the Prairie Inn?" Pa wiped a piece of bread around his plate, sopping up the grey-brown gravy that had remained behind.

He folded the wet bread and bit off a big chunk.

"Yes." Ma glanced at me and hesitated before saying, "Of course, I didn't say anything but there was lots I could have."

Pa raised an eyebrow. "Such as…what?" he asked.

"You know perfectly well what." Ma stopped speaking and took another look in my direction. A slight frown creased her forehead. "Enough dawdling, Luke. You finish up your dinner."

The chunks of liver that were still on my plate had turned cold and had taken on a green sheen, making them even less appealing than when they'd been served. I stuck my fork into one and lifted it toward my mouth. Ma's eyes followed every move I made.

I touched the edge of the meat to my mouth and felt my stomach lurch. With some effort, I forced my lips apart but I just couldn't seem to make myself take the bite.

"It's cold," I said.

"It's only cold because you *let* it get cold."

There was no point in protesting any further. Any minute my father would speak up. Then I'd have no choice but to shove that cold, disgusting lump into my mouth.

The Glory Wind

And then, a miracle! With a warning that I'd get nothing before breakfast, I was released!

It was too easy, but I was so happy to escape the liver that I didn't stop to wonder why until later. When I did, I realized that they'd let me off because they wanted to talk about something they didn't want me to hear.

Something to do with Raedine Moor and her new job.

Chapter Three

The Prairie Inn is a three-storey building in the centre of town. Except for the grain elevators, which are clustered on the west edge of Junction, the inn is the tallest building there. Hank's Barber Shop, the Post Office, Clive's General Store, Lidgate's Farming Supplies, and a few others are just squatting around it along the main street.

Being taller than the stores isn't the only thing that sets it apart from the buildings around it. For one thing, the inn is made of stone while the other structures are all wood. I got some of the history of its construction one afternoon when we were in town.

Pa and I were sitting in the cab of our one-ton pickup truck—a 1939 Dodge TD-21 that we'd bought second-hand the summer before. We had the windows down to let in whatever breeze might happen along, and to clear out the smell of fuel. Pa had filled the tank earlier and had sloshed a little gasoline on his boots.

It was before the Moors came, when you could still mention the Inn without that cold feeling in your core. I made some observation, now long forgotten, about the place.

"You might care to know, Luke, that some of the stone—not the main part, but some—was imported," Pa said, gesturing toward the inn. "For instance, the red stones—those are Tennessee marble. The original owners had them brought in from the Appalachians.

"It seems they set out with big dreams—bigger'n their purse, as it happened. Made fools of themselves telling everyone hereabouts that the main structure was going to be some kind of fancy stone from Texas. Then, suddenly, it was never mentioned again. I'd say they found out the cost was too high. In the end, they used Tyndall stone from Garson, right here in Manitoba. It's a fine quality limestone, but all their boasting took away from it."

Even so, it was easily the most fancy place in Junction. Of course, there wasn't much competition from the stores, which are all plain and box-like, sporting signs that look as tired and faded as most of the people who run them.

Valerie Sherrard

There's no sign on the Prairie Inn. Instead, its name is carved deep in a huge slab of rock that forms the header over the double doors. That and heavy, blood-red curtains make it look rich and classy. I'd never been in there, but I'd heard my mother say that if the *church* had the proper support, it could have velvet curtains like the *inn* has.

Aside from those few details, I'd never given the place much thought before Gracie and her mom came to Junction. That changed almost the minute Raedine got a job there. Then, the whole town took notice. Talk burst into the air like an overripe cattail, exploding and floating about, each bit of it a tiny part of the whole.

It might have gone right by me if the voices hadn't dropped to a hush whenever the subject of Raedine's job came up. That could mean only one thing—that, as Ma says, it was none of my business. The second I picked up on that, I became immediately and keenly interested.

I began gathering bits of the talk, putting it together like a puzzle. Only it seemed there were layers and levels to the story that made it harder to figure out than any other town gossip I'd come across.

I was in a good position to gather information on account of we lived next door to the Moors. That gave some of the local ladies the idea that my mother would know all about it.

They started arriving at our door on the flimsiest excuses, each of them grilling Ma in her own way. Some were bold enough to come right out and ask what they wanted to know.

"What in the name of time is that woman *thinking*, taking a job in a place like that?" my mother's cousin, Cora Deighton, asked. Then, without waiting for an answer, she rushed on. "Don't tell me she can't look around her and see what's going on!"

"I'm sure she has plenty of other things on her mind," Ma said.

"She has eyes, doesn't she?" Cora rolled her own as she asked.

"She's new in town and a widow," Ma said. Blotchy red spots were growing on her cheeks. "It seems only fair to give her the benefit of the doubt."

"Oh, I gave her the benefit of the doubt when I first heard, but she's been there for going on two weeks now, and if she hasn't noticed that there's not a single self-respecting woman working there, then she's either blind or a fool."

"Whatever she has or hasn't noticed," Ma countered, "I

suppose her biggest worry is being able to feed her child."

"I'd let my child starve right to death before I'd work in a place that's little better than a…" Here, Cora glanced about and lowered her voice.

I had to strain to hear (from my hiding place behind the wood-box) and at the time I thought she'd said *bottle*. I spent a good many hours trying to make sense of how anyone could think a big building like that was no better than a bottle, and even if that was true, why it was so terrible for Raedine to be working there.

Of course, I now know she said *brothel*, but that word hadn't yet reached my eleven-year-old ears. That was unfortunate, since Cora Deighton was one of the most outspoken women around. I knew that if anyone was likely to clear up the mystery with some blunt remark, it would be her. The confusion over thinking she'd said *bottle* made it that much harder for me to figure out what was so terrible about Raedine working at the Prairie Inn.

Most of the ladies took a more roundabout route than Cora had, disguising their curiosity as Christian concern.

"Now you know I'm not one to put my nose where it doesn't belong," Evelyn Fuller insisted as she shifted her baby from one hip to the other, "but a person feels a kind of obligation in a situation like this."

"You're right, of course," Ma answered. "We should all get together and do what we can to help."

Our visitor faltered ever so slightly. "You mean, go to talk to her as...uh...a group?"

"*Talk* to her?" Ma repeated. "I can't see what help talking would be. I was thinking more of offering to watch Gracie—that's her daughter—when Raedine has to work, or taking her food and things for the house and such. Like we did for Jimmy Pafford when his wife passed on last year."

"Well, I didn't quite mean..." Mrs. Fuller voice trailed off and confusion clouded her face with an uncertainty that she tried to hide with a bright smile. She stammered a little and then told Ma that of course she'd do her part.

Meanwhile, the baby on her hip—a girl, by the look of the bonnet—was leaning over sideways. A long line of drool hung from her mouth and I poked my head out just a tad, in order to watch it break away and hit the floor.

It was a mistake. The baby spied me and a grin spread over her face at the discovery. I frowned at her fiercely, thinking that might discourage her but that effort backfired. She reacted with delight and began to bounce and chortle and wave her fists about.

I ducked down and squeezed back into the corner, even though my mother and Mrs. Fuller weren't looking in my direction. I stayed very still and tried to breathe quietly, though it sounded loud and rasping as it reached my ears.

Luckily, no one paid her any mind and eventually my heart settled back to normal. Even so, I didn't relax completely until Mrs Fuller had taken the thread she came to borrow, along with her drooling baby, and gone home.

Chapter Four

Carmella Tait is a large coloured woman—the only coloured person in town. She's also my friend.

Carmella did a lot of canning and preserving. More often than not, if she was in her kitchen, she'd be peeling something, seated at the scarred wooden table, her ample hips spilling out over the sides of the chair. The blade of her paring knife would be jutting out from the chubby cave of her brown hand, gliding over the surface of some vegetable or other while skins fell away into a slop bucket for the pigs.

Usually, she was singing too. Carmella had a powerful voice, though she couldn't carry a tune at all, and she loved to sing hymns just as loud as she could manage. I was used to having the off-key sounds of her faith float out to meet me on my way to her door.

When I was small, I had the idea that there was something faintly magical about Carmella's house. Even though it was one of the poorer homes in town, there was always a certain feeling there, a feeling that could go right through you if you stayed for any time at all. It was a bit like the warmth that soaks into you when you lie out in the sun—a lazy, pleasant sense that things are just fine.

I wondered if other people felt it too, but it wasn't in my nature to ask. And the idea of sharing my own private thoughts never crossed my mind.

Of course, it wasn't the house at all.

* * *

Gracie met Carmella soon after coming to Junction, and all because of a skunk.

It began the way pretty much every visit to the Taits' place did, with an errand for my mother. That was a new responsibility for me—being sent to pick up an ingredient for something Ma was cooking, or for one of Carmella's remedies for a toothache or sick stomach or the like.

I normally enjoyed going, but on this particular occasion I wasn't so keen when my mother called out for me.

"Luke!"

I knew immediately that she was going to send me on an

errand. There was a certain sound in her voice whenever she wanted me to fetch or deliver something. And like I said, under most circumstances, I'd have been glad to go, but this time Gracie was coming over. She'd said so the last time I'd seen her. She'd said it in the way she always did: not as a question or a request, but as an announcement.

In the few short weeks I'd known her, Gracie's announcements had cast some sort of spell on me. Everything she said came out large and grand. I had the feeling that she was willing things into happening just by saying them. It intrigued me and I found myself thinking about her more than I'd ever thought about anything else.

So when my mother summoned me that morning, I didn't answer her right away. Instead, I stood very still and silent, hoping that she'd get distracted with something else and forget that she wanted me.

She called a second time, her voice more insistent. At that point I knew I'd better answer, or else. If she had to call me a third time, she'd be angry. She'd know I'd heard her and that my failure to answer had been deliberate.

I called out that I was coming and ran down the stairs and into the kitchen.

"I want you to go over to the Taits' house and see if

Carmella has a dozen eggs she can sell me," Ma said. "That horrid skunk got into the henhouse again and there's not a single egg left there."

"Do I have to go right now?" I asked.

"Well, of course. Why on earth would I call you if I didn't want you to go now?" Ma nodded toward the table where a dime sat waiting. "There's the money to pay her. And don't dawdle."

I looked grudgingly at the dime. "But Gracie is coming over," I said.

Ma crossed her arms over her chest and gave me a long, hard look. "Well then," she said at last, "you go on out to the field and tell your father that I need him to go get me some eggs because you're just too busy to do it for me."

"I'm going," I grumbled. I walked past her to get the dime, cringing because she still had her arms folded, and that cross look was hovering on her face.

I let the screen door bang behind me, its wooden clatter setting up a rhythm that went on in my head after the door had come to a wobbling halt. Crossing the yard, I kicked the heads off some dandelions and stomped on a scurrying ant.

I'd just rounded the shed when I saw Gracie running toward the house, her hair rising and falling as her feet pounded dust up from the path. Just a little ways beyond her, Raedine was following, a basket swinging from one hand.

"Gracie!" I shouted. "I'm over here!"

She turned, shielding her eyes with a sort of salute, and scanned the yard until she spied me. Her arm shot up in a wave and a smile burst onto her face.

"I brought my mom with me," she yelled.

I ran to meet Gracie and walked to the house with her, just a little ahead of Raedine. Ma scowled slightly at my reappearance but hid it when she saw that we had company.

"Gracie and her mom are here," I said.

"Well, what a nice surprise," Ma said with a smile. "Come on in, Raedine."

She remembered the eggs then and asked Raedine if it would be all right for Gracie to go with me to get them. Raedine said it was fine and Gracie and I were out the door and running across the yard in a flash.

It was a long way to the Taits' house if you went by the road, but only about a mile if you cut through the spring barley fields. We followed the path I always took, making our way along the edges of the crops.

There was a slight breeze, the dancing kind that makes

a prairie crop ripple, like shimmering green waves racing over the heads of the grain. Without warning, Gracie stopped, staring at them, transfixed.

She said nothing. Her breath slowed and deepened until I became aware of it to the exclusion of all other sounds. A small hand rose from her side and travelled across the space between us, found mine and took hold of it as though it was the most natural thing in the world.

I'd never held hands with a girl before. Once the shock wore off I realized it wasn't entirely unpleasant. And besides, no one could see us out there in the field, which is why I decided not to pull my hand away.

I snuck a few cautious glances at Gracie's face, mostly focusing on her eyes, which were full and shining as she stared out over the field. Her head began to move ever so slightly, following the sway of the grain. Within a moment or two her body was moving to and fro as well, and then she tugged her hand free and stretched it out in a motion that looked, for all the world, as though she was stroking the top of the field.

"Do you think," she said suddenly, "that the field is green where they buried my daddy?"

"Sure," I said. "They always bury people in green fields.

I think it's some kind of a rule."

She nodded. "I don't quite seem to know *why* my daddy died in the war," she said.

"I guess his time had come," I told her wisely. I'd heard Pastor Lockhart say that at funerals for some of the Junction men who had gone off to fight and not returned.

Gracie didn't speak for a moment. I was searching through my head, trying to find something on the subject that might be helpful, but when she spoke again, all she said was, "I guess we better go get those eggs for your mother."

Chapter Five

We headed off again, and by and by we reached Carmella's house. Strains of a song I couldn't identify met us as we reached the door and knocked. The singing stopped long enough for Carmella to tell us to come in and then picked right back up and finished out a couple more lines before coming to a halt. Carmella clasped a hand over her bosom at the end, the blade of her knife pressing into the flowered fabric of her housedress.

"You'll just have to excuse me," she said. "Those songs about Canaan always seem to clutch tight onto my heart. But what's this? I see you've brought along a friend."

"Yes'm," I said quickly. "This here's Gracie Moor. She just moved to Junction, right next door to my place."

"Is that right? Well, bless your heart, Gracie. I'm Carmella Tait. You can just call me Carmella."

"Hi," Gracie said. "What's a *Canaan*?"

"Canaan? Why, it's the land of milk and honey, of course. Don't you go to Sunday School?"

Gracie frowned, not in a cross way, but the way you do when you're thinking hard about something. "I guess I don't need to," she said at last.

"Don't need to! Child, everybody needs to know the Good Lord, and Sunday School is a fine place to make His acquaintance."

"Is that where God lives?" Gracie wanted to know.

"Well, no. God is everywhere."

"Then why do I need to go to church to meet Him?"

Carmella paused. The strip of skin hanging from the potato she was peeling stopped growing. She shook her head a little and then lifted it to meet Gracie's eyes. "It's not my place to tell someone else's child what to do."

"Okay," Gracie said.

"Anyway," Carmella's smile reappeared, "welcome to Junction. I remember it like it was yesterday—the day I first came here. I was so excited!"

"How long have you lived here?" Gracie asked.

"Matter of fact," Carmella told her, "I've been here exactly the same length of time Luke has."

"Eleven years?" I asked.

"Be twelve years come October 15," she said.

"That's my birthday!" I said.

"I *know* that's your birthday, child. Why else would I say that I've been here *exactly* the same time as you? The day you were born is the very day I came to Junction, a new bride." Carmella turned to Gracie.

"It raised a bit of a stir when we stepped off that train, let me tell you. I don't think the people around here were quite ready to see a white man—and one of their own at that—married to a coloured woman. And I imagine we made a sight all right, Mr. Tait as thin as a pin and so frail looking, hobbling around on that wooden leg, with his new bride—a round young darkie. Him, past forty while I was barely into my twenties."

This startled me, mostly because Ma had told me it wasn't polite to say "darkie" or "negro," only "coloured." I decided it must be all right for Carmella to say, since she was talking about herself.

"There were a few things said outright, but mostly folks judged quietly behind their smiles. I could see it in their faces. Only I didn't mind. I was just happy to have a home of my own at last."

The Glory Wind

"Where'd you live before you came here?" Gracie asked.

"Nebraska. Lived there from the time I was a little girl. My mother and father—John and Bella Quartermaine—both died before I was nine, and I stayed with my brother and his wife and their children for the next five years. I'm grateful that they took me in, but it wasn't a happy time.

"When I was fourteen I went to work for the Hammonds, a well-to-do family in Gosper County. I worked there for three years, until one day they accused me of stealing from them and let me go."

"*Did* you steal from them?" Gracie asked, wide-eyed at the thought.

"Land alive, of course I didn't! It was their oldest boy. Gone bad, that one."

"Didn't you tell them it was really him?" Gracie's hands had flown to her hips and her face was full of indignation.

"You think they'd be taking my side over their own flesh and blood? I just packed up my things and moved along. Got myself a job working in the laundry at the county hospital and found a room in a boarding house. I shared it with another coloured gal, an older woman named Dorothy Fuggins. She had a weakness for bourbon, though if you knew her story you'd find it hard to condemn her. Overall,

I don't suppose it was too bad, those years of living at the boarding house."

Carmella paused, as she often did when she was telling a story. I was used to waiting but Gracie wasn't inclined toward a lot of patience. I doubt a full minute had gone by before she burst out saying, "Well, go on! What happened then?"

Carmella looked a mite startled, but then she chuckled and patted Gracie's hand and continued with her account. "Then Mr. Tait came along. It was his cousin who ran the boarding house, and he had stopped in for a few days on his way back from visiting his brother in Missouri.

"One night I was hanging some washing out back where the lines were and Mr. Tait was out there, sitting and enjoying his pipe. We got to talking and then he asked me to sit with him for a spell. And somehow, the next few evenings we found ourselves sitting and talking—and then on the fourth night he asked me would I like to marry an older man with one leg and go to live in Canada, and I said I sure enough would."

Carmella paused and cleared her throat. "So Mr. Tait delayed his return for a few days and we found a preacher who would marry us. Then we came straight on up here."

The Glory Wind

"Do you have any children?" Gracie asked, looking around as though Carmella's offspring might materialize just from being mentioned.

"No, child, there are just the two of us rattling around in this big old house. That's my cross to bear," Carmella sighed heavily. "It cheers my heart when Luke here comes to visit, and I hope you'll do the same—with or without him."

And then, rather to my surprise, Gracie launched herself forward, threw her arms around Carmella's broad shoulders, and hugged her with a fierce passion.

PART TWO

The Calm Before the Storm

Most people think that tornados come with some kind of warning—hail, lightning, certain patterns of rain, or even complete silence. The truth is, tornados are trickier than that. Sometimes one or more of those things comes along beforehand and gives you a hint, but other times there's no clue at all. You're just going about your normal routine, and then, without warning, *wham*!

Chapter Six

Summer is my favourite time of year. I love it when the sun hangs high overhead and the hours unfold like a lazy Sunday drive on a prairie road.

I had chores, of course. That started from the time I was big enough to walk. I did lots of things, like bringing in armloads of kindling for the stove, scattering feed about for the chickens, and running errands for Ma.

This still left the vast majority of my time for me to fill as best I could, and as an only child (a rare thing in Junction) I was left to find ways to amuse myself. Aside from the odd day spent at Keane Dempsey's place, I mostly just kicked around by myself. Until, that is, Gracie moved in next door. All of a sudden, I went from spending a lot of time alone to having a nearly constant companion.

Our mothers were clearly happy about the idea of us spending time together. Apparently, there's a certain amount of worry involved when you have a kid wandering alone in the fields all summer long. Not that there was much danger—the odd rattlesnake would be about the worst and they were far from common.

For Ma, the biggest concern was that I'd twist an ankle or break a leg. "Mind you watch and don't step in any holes," she'd tell me. "You crack a bone and you'll be sitting out there hurting something dreadful—under the blazing sun too, until the buzzards get you. Be nothing but bleached bones by the time anyone happens to find you."

"Oh, Alice, don't be telling the boy such nonsense," Pa would say if he happened to be around. It was one of the few things my parents ever argued about, at least when I was in hearing range. My father didn't want my mother turning me into some kind of sissy while my mother hoped for my father's sake that he'd never have to know the grief of finding out she'd been right all along.

"I'll be careful," I'd promise her, though the truth was, once I got out there, wandering and exploring, I never gave a thought to watching where I was going. There were lots of times when I stumbled and went sprawling over rocks or prairie dog holes. Now and then I hurt myself bad enough that I'd have cried if I'd been a girl, but never to the point where I got any kind of fright out of it.

Ma would dab Mercurochrome on any scrapes I brought home and it surprised me how readily she believed I'd scratched myself on a bush when the injury was clearly caused by a fall. I wondered about that some, but I've never had much luck figuring my mother out.

Anyway, after Raedine and Gracie moved into the house on the next property, there was someone to prowl about the fields with. It was a relief to Ma to know I had someone with me who could come fetch her when I broke my leg and was sitting out there waiting for the buzzards to arrive.

Raedine had been having trouble finding a sitter to watch Gracie while she was at work all day and Ma told her there was no need of that; Gracie could come over to our place for Raedine's shifts for the rest of the summer. Raedine insisted she would pay, but Ma said she wouldn't hear of it and if a person couldn't be allowed to do something neighbourly, she didn't know what the world was coming to. Raedine cried a little and that seemed to settle it.

After that, Gracie would show up at our place every morning about nine o'clock. Raedine's shift at the Prairie Inn started at ten, so she'd set out walking into town around the time Gracie came over. Most days someone would stop and give her a lift.

Gracie almost always wore skirts with pockets large enough to hold the waxed-paper-wrapped sandwich she brought along for lunch, even though Ma kept telling her that wasn't necessary and land sakes we could certainly give her a sandwich.

I'd pack a lunch up too and we'd head out, with Ma in the background telling us to mind we didn't both step in a hole at once.

There's a special kind of joy in having a warm summer day stretching out ahead of you. It feels endless and full of promise. And the strange thing is that even if nothing happens all day it leaves you feeling totally satisfied.

I had many such days before Gracie came along, but they were spent quite differently from those we shared that summer. I'd never been a particularly imaginative kid, and I'd generally just amble about, wandering the fields or wooded groves in a sort of aimless exploration.

I could spend whole days examining clusters of anthills, offering the ants crumbs from my overall pockets, where I frequently carried a biscuit or the heel from a loaf of bread to eat during my travels. These snacks often ended up crumbled from being squashed against me when I climbed trees or lay out flat on the ground to watch the activity of some bug or animal I'd spied.

Other times I might start some ambitious project, like the days I spent working on building a rock fort. Hours and hours were devoted to lugging the biggest stones I could carry and arranging them in a relatively straight row until I had erected the eight-inch high beginning of a single wall. By then, my enthusiasm for the fort was spent.

Still, a boy with a pile of rocks is rarely without a plan, and after several other failed projects, I'd built something that vaguely resembled a chair.

Gracie laughed the first time she saw it. "Did you make that?" she asked, as though there was a chance it might have just happened on its own.

I mumbled something and hoped she'd drop it.

Not Gracie. "It's all wrong!" she said.

"It looks okay to me," I grumbled. It was hard to stay cross, though. Gracie was standing next to me, leaning toward the rock chair, and the breeze was blowing the soft curls of her hair against my arm.

"Is it supposed to be a throne?" she asked, sounding doubtful.

"No, a chair," I said. The words weren't even all the way out of my mouth when I wished I'd lied. A throne sounded so much better.

"A *chair*?" Gracie repeated. It was clear from her tone that she couldn't possibly have been less impressed.

"I was making a wall at the start," I told her.

"A *wall*?" she echoed, her voice even more incredulous. "*Why?*"

"I just wanted to make something."

"A wall in a field," she said. She seemed unable to grasp the idea.

"Well, it was going to be a fort," I explained. "That was just the first wall."

"Oh, a *fort*." That seemed to make more sense to her. At least, she nodded and stopped looking as though I was a rabid gopher or something. "Well, you don't have enough for that."

"So? What would you have made?" I asked. I wasn't really interested in her ideas. I just doubted she'd come up with anything that was any good, and then I could make fun of her the way she'd done with me.

Gracie pondered. She stared at the rocks, frowning while she thought. Then her face lit up and she shouted,

"A Circle of Truth!"

"A what?"

"A circle where you can only tell the truth, no matter what. But you're never, *ever* allowed to tell anybody else anything you hear in there."

I was still turning the idea over in my head when Gracie started pulling rocks out of place, taking down the chair. I jumped in, doing the same, yanking hard on them so she'd see that I could handle the task better than some scrawny girl.

"I'll get the big ones," I told her.

"There *are* no big ones," she answered.

"Well, I couldn't find any *really* big ones," I said. "But some of 'em are heavier than they look."

Gracie shrugged and went back to what she was doing. For a few moments the only sounds were those of the rocks clacking together as we dismantled the stone chair.

"My best friend's name is Karly," Gracie blurted suddenly. "Karly Grasse. Only, I don't know if I'll get to see her again, since she still lives…in my old town, and I live here now."

"Where is your old town?" I asked.

"Far, far away," she told me. "It took us more than half a

day just to drive here. We weren't driving the whole entire time, though. We had to stop to get gas and food and use the fast-ill-a-tease,"

"What's a fast-ill-a-tease?"

"It's another name for a bathroom. Every time we stopped somewhere my mom asked for the key so we could use the fast-ill-a-tease."

I nodded, like I'd just remembered exactly what that was. "Oh, yeah," I said.

"But that's not the important part," she said, giving me a stern look. "I was telling you about my friend Karly."

"Right," I said. "Because you don't know when you'll see her again."

"Or *if* I'll see her again," Gracie corrected.

"You might," I offered uselessly.

"I don't know," she said. She'd gotten very still, which somehow made her face look solemn and small.

"When you get older you can get a job and buy your own car and drive to where she lives."

"Cars cost a lot of money."

"You think I don't know that?" I scoffed. "My Pa showed me a picture of a car that cost more than two thousand dollars. But you don't have to buy a new one."

"How much is one that isn't new?"

"Maybe a couple hundred dollars or something."

"That's still an awful lot." Gracie sank down onto a rock, looking defeated.

"Or you can go on the train!" I said.

"The train," echoed Gracie.

"Then you only need to buy a ticket and that's all."

Gracie jumped back to her feet and threw her arms around me. I shrugged them off as quick as lightning, but that didn't seem to bother her.

"You saved my heart from breaking right in two—thinking about never seeing Karly again," she said.

"Your heart can't break in two just because of not seeing somebody," I said.

I thought it was true.

Chapter Seven

We spent more time in the Circle of Truth than anywhere else that first summer. It was a safe place, on account of the rule about things being secret. We'd stretch out on our backs and look up at the wide open sky and just free all the thoughts and ideas that wanted to float out of our mouths.

The circle is about fifteen feet across with a really big rock in the centre. That one was thanks to Carmella's husband, Clarence Tait, who brought over his old workhorse one afternoon and hauled it from another field for us.

"What'd you say this here thing is for?" he asked, surveying the stones we'd spread about in a circular formation.

"It's a Circle of Truth," Gracie told him. "It has special powers."

"Izzat right?" he said, while a sprig of foxtail barley

waved at us from the corner of his mouth. "And what exactly is it that gives it these powers?"

"The circle part," Gracie explained patiently. "Everyone knows that circles are powerful."

"Izzat right, now?" He shook his head like it was a bit too much for him. "Well, you youngsters enjoy it. I got to be gettin' back home."

We thanked him and stood watching while he hoisted himself onto the horse and swung his wooden leg over its wide midsection. A low, grumbling sound came from his throat, which started the horse lumbering along.

"I wonder why Carmella calls him Mr. Tait instead of his first name," Gracie pondered as the horse and rider grew smaller in the distance.

"I dunno."

"But don't you *wonder*?"

"Why would I wonder about that?"

"It doesn't seem that you wonder about *anything*," Gracie sighed. She'd gotten in the habit of sighing whenever I said or did something puzzling or exasperating. She sighed a lot that first summer.

"I guess I'm not a curious person," I said.

"*Karly* was curious," Gracie said.

The Glory Wind

"*So?*" I'd gotten tired of the regular comparisons to Karly. "She's a girl. Like you."

"And just what do you mean by that, Luke Haliwell?"

"Nuthin'." As often happened with Gracie, my courage disappeared at the sight of her blazing eyes.

But as the weeks went by, Karly was mentioned less and less. I can't say I minded that, though I don't think it had yet occurred to me that Gracie and I had become best friends. In fact, I might have socked you in the eye if you'd suggested such a thing to me. Best friends with a girl! The idea was ridiculous.

So I was in for a bit of an eye-opener one day late in August. Gracie and I were walking down the road alongside the fence that runs the length of Guthrie's farm. That's across the road from the house where Gracie and her mom lived.

We'd been ambling along, looking for un-scavenged blueberry bushes, when Keane Dempsey came riding up on his bike, kicking up a cloud of dust and pebbles behind him. He drove straight to where Gracie and I were standing, reversing on the pedal just in time to stop before he ran right into us.

"Hey, Luke," he said, "You can come over to my place

if you want."

"I'm kinda busy," I said.

He looked surprised—and not exactly pleased. "I thought we could do some of the stuff in the Keds Handbook," he said. "My mom said we could use her stamp pad to make fingerprints, like the book says."

"We were looking for blueberries," I told him.

"*Blueberries!*" he scoffed. "Big deal. We can…" Here, Keane paused and looked at Gracie like he'd just noticed her. "Hey, she can come too, and we can do some magic tricks for her."

"Okay," Gracie said, and it was settled. It seemed that if Gracie decided something, that was it. (This was rarely true for things I decided.)

As we walked to Keane's place he told Gracie how amazed and impressed she was going to be when she saw the magic tricks he could do. He said she'd probably never seen a magician who could do those kinds of things, and he sternly warned her that he couldn't reveal his secrets so there was no point in her even asking.

When we got there Keane told Gracie to sit and wait by the woodpile. "We need some stuff for the magic," he said, grabbing my arm and pulling me along.

The Glory Wind

I glanced over my shoulder to see Gracie standing still and looking straight at me. I couldn't read the expression on her face. I wanted to say, "I'll be right back," or "Watch out for hornets," or something, but my mind was blank. So I turned around and followed Keane inside without a word.

It took a good twenty minutes for Keane to gather up the things he needed to perform the tricks in the Keds Handbook, and when we went back outside Gracie was nowhere to be seen.

"Now where'd that dumb old girl go to?" Keane grumbled, worried he'd been cheated out of an audience.

"I'm not a dumb old girl and you take that back or I won't watch your magic show!"

We both turned at the sound of her voice and saw Gracie coming along the path from the outhouse.

"Well?" she demanded, hands on her hips and arms folded out like wings. "Are you going to take it back?"

"I thought you took off is all," he muttered.

"So do you take it back?"

"Yeah, yeah."

Looking at Keane's face I almost laughed out loud. He was beat and he knew it, but strangely enough, he didn't seem to mind all that much. Then it hit me that that was exactly what I'd felt so many times in the few weeks I'd known Gracie. You knew you weren't going to win any arguments with her, not only because you couldn't—but because deep inside you didn't honestly want to.

Keane did the tricks while I played the parts he'd given me when we were inside—announcing each of the acts and making comments like "Isn't that amazing?" and "How does he do it, folks?" and such.

"Keane will now perform the Marvellous Match-Mending trick!" I boomed as he produced one of his mother's handkerchiefs and waved it about dramatically.

Gracie watched, as she had each of the preceding feats, with intent interest, her eyes following every move he made as he produced a match and tucked it into the handkerchief's folds.

"We'll need a volunteer from our audience!" I declared.

Gracie raised her hand obediently as she had done each time a volunteer had been required.

"You! The young lady in the front row. Come on up and join us here on stage," I instructed.

Gracie crossed the few feet of ground separating us and waited for further instructions.

The Glory Wind

Keane took over at that point, thrusting the hanky toward her and asking if she could feel the match in there. Gracie nodded as her fingers felt the small wooden stick through the thin fabric. Then Keane told her to break it in two and she obliged with a brisk snap.

"You sure you busted it?" he asked.

Gracie nodded, her eyes never leaving the handkerchief, over which Keane proceeded to mutter his own magic spell of za-wowie-powie. When he opened it and produced a fully intact match, Gracie's eyes grew rounder and she smiled and clapped. It was all I could do not to blurt out that the match she'd broken was a different one, that Keane had hidden it in the hanky's hem beforehand.

After Keane had finished showing off with the tricks, he decided Gracie would probably like to see some of the feats of strength that were in the handbook.

"I'm pretty strong," he boasted.

But just then I remembered Ma had mentioned that she'd like me and Gracie to take some quilting patches to Carmella one day this week. All of a sudden it felt like something that needed to be done right away. I told Keane we had to go.

He suggested that it would be okay if Gracie wanted to

hang around and watch him put on a strong man show, on account of he was even bored enough to let a girl hang around for a while.

"Mrs. Haliwell is watching me while my mother is at work," Gracie told him, "so I have to stay with Luke."

We left then. On one hand, I was happy that she wasn't staying behind. On the other hand, I was out-of-sorts because the only reason she'd come along with me was that she thought she had no other choice.

We were about halfway to my place when I couldn't stand it anymore. "Why don't you just go on back to Keane's house if you want to."

"Back to Keane's house?" Gracie echoed. Her voice and face were both surprised as can be. "Why would I want to do that?"

"I just thought you might," I said.

Gracie shook her head. "Keane is okay and all, but he has an awfully big opinion of himself."

I think, if I had to pin it down, that would be the moment I realized Gracie had become the only person I really wanted to be around.

Chapter Eight

During the summer, I don't see much of my pals from school. Most of them live on farms on the north side of town and that's too far to walk both ways in a day. Sundays are about the only time I get to see some of the other kids. The Presbyterians, anyway, and sometimes the Mennonites, since their church is only a few minutes' walk down the road.

There's Johnny Oak, whose father owns the biggest piece of land around here; Alex Filmon, the only boy in a family of nine; Teddy Tompkins, whose two older brothers went to war and never came back; and William Northcott, the loudest kid I ever met.

Teddy was the only one besides me to have met Gracie before school let in for the fall. Seems he'd been dragged along when his mother went to call on Raedine, to welcome her to Junction.

"All they did was sit and bawl for about an hour," Teddy reported. "Good thing my Pa wasn't there. He says talking doesn't change anything, or bring anyone back."

"Was Gracie at home?" I asked.

"Yeah. She's pretty bossy," he said. "I feel sorry for you, living next to them, with all that bawling and bossing going on full time."

"Well, she doesn't boss *me* around," I claimed, knowing that it was a lie and I was telling it right there in the churchyard.

The truth was, I was facing a problem that was a lot bigger than Gracie's bossiness. I'd been thinking about it quite a bit as September crept closer and closer, and it was worrying me a good deal.

Brandon Jackson and Pete West are my best friends at school. We've chummed together through the years and, like all the other boys in our grade, we had little use for girls. Their row of desks sat facing ours across the classroom, but they might as well have been across the ocean for all the interest we had in them.

We'd known them, right from the first grade, as bizarre and annoying creatures. They were quick to cry or accuse and the games they played were dull and silly. For the most part, we acted like they didn't even exist.

Girls, on the other hand, made it only too clear that *they* were aware of *us*. They did it with disgusted sounds like "*Eww*" or muffled whispers that came from hand-covered mouths. You could pretty much count on either of those things being followed by an outburst of giggles. Sometimes, they'd even run off, as though we were chasing them, which was never the case.

I didn't even want to think about the reaction I'd get from the other boys if they saw that I was friends with Gracie. It's one thing to spend time with a girl if you're forced to, but no one in my grade would go making a fool of himself by chumming with a girl (and one in grade six, at that) when there were boys around. I wasn't about to be the first.

The problem I couldn't seem to settle in my mind was how I was going to talk about it to Gracie. Of course, I still wanted to be friends with her, just not at school. Somehow, I didn't picture her taking that very well. As the days got closer and closer to the start of school, my nerves were near frazzled from the worry of it, and I still hadn't found the courage to bring it up with her. Oh, I'd tried a couple of times, but the words wouldn't come out and I kept putting it off.

And then there were no more days to put it off *to* because school was starting the next day. Gracie was at our place as usual, while Raedine was at work, and we were sitting on the fence to the south of the barn. Gracie was chattering away but I wasn't really paying attention, since I was straining my brain trying to think of a way to bring up the subject without making her madder than a swatted nest of hornets.

I felt kind of the way I did the time our family went to Grand Beach for the day, and I swam out too far and went under. I was floundering around underwater, desperate for something to grab onto to save myself, and knowing full well there was nothing. The more I panicked, the worse it got, until I was upside down, with only my foot sticking out of the water. It was a stranger who saved me that day— taking hold of my flailing foot and pulling me up and out just before the bursting in my chest would have forced me to take in water.

I didn't figure anyone was going to come along and rescue me this time, but I was wrong. About mid-afternoon a truck came chugging along the road. As it got close I could see that it was Mr. Tait's and, when it was near enough, that Carmella was seated beside him in the cab.

The Glory Wind

It slowed down and pulled up to a stop about parallel with where Gracie and I were sitting. The door opened and Carmella swung herself sideways and made a little hop down. She turned and said something to her husband and closed the door.

Mr. Tait raised his hand to us before pulling back onto the road and driving off.

"Hi Carmella!" Gracie called. She was already down off the fence and running toward our visitor, her hair bouncing along like it was chasing her.

Carmella's throaty laugh floated to me as she reached down and met Gracie with a wide-armed hug. I took my time getting there. Once Carmella starts hugging people, there's no stopping her.

Sure enough, she grabbed me and squeezed me as soon as I was close enough. "Just look at you," she said, though I don't see how she *could*—what with me crushed against her bosom that way. "Off to school to start grade seven tomorrow. How the years have gone by."

Next thing, as if she'd read my mind about not being able to see me, she thrust me away from her, her hands holding onto my shoulders while she looked me up and down.

"My, my, but I think you're taller every time I see you," she said. "And handsome! I declare, you surely are turning into a fine-looking boy."

This set Gracie to giggling, which Carmella seemed to find a mite insulting. "Don't you think Luke is handsome, Gracie?"

Gracie rolled her eyes and laughed some more.

"Well, now, you might want to be careful what you say, missy," Carmella said with a shake of her head. "Could be that you'll grow up and want to marry this very boy. I've seen it happen before."

"Well, if I ever *wanted* to marry him, then I would," Gracie said, "but I don't mean to get married at all."

"*No?*" Carmella seemed quite amazed by this. I, on the other hand, was feeling something peculiar, which I figure must have been relief.

"No!" declared Gracie, and that, thankfully, seemed to end the discussion. We started toward the house as if someone had suggested it, though no one had.

"I suppose you two are wondering what brings me here today," Carmella said.

"What?" Gracie and I asked together.

"School!" Carmella said, like she was announcing that

we'd won a prize. "And I have something for you."

Well! That got our attention all right. We took turns guessing what it might be until we reached the back door. Gracie guessed hair ribbons and clips; I thought it might be a super-sized eraser or an Indian rubber ball, but Carmella just shook her head and laughed.

"Carmella!" my mother said as we trooped into her kitchen. "What a nice surprise. Come right on in."

"Afternoon, Alice," Carmella said. "I just came by to give Luke and Gracie here a little something for the first day of school."

"Well, isn't that kind of you!" Ma said. "You'll have a cup of tea, won't you?"

"I never say no to a cup of tea," Carmella said, settling herself onto a chair at the table. "Now, I best give these children their presents before they climb right up on my lap."

Gracie and I laughed at that, but we backed off a bit. I guess we were kind of crowding her, but it's hard waiting on a surprise.

Chapter Nine

We didn't have to wait any longer because Carmella reached into the big purse she carried everywhere she went, and came out with two pencil boxes, one for each of us. I could see right off that she'd made them herself, and when she passed me mine I said, "Oh!" right out loud. The wooden sliding piece that opened the case had my name and an eagle's likeness carved and painted on it. It was the nicest pencil box I'd ever seen.

Gracie seemed just as thrilled with hers. She was holding it at arm's length, staring at it, but when she saw me looking over she turned it around so I could see it too. Her name was there, of course, and beside that was a cluster of prairie crocus in full bloom.

"Oh, Carmella, it's so beautiful! And how did you know that this is my favourite flower ever?" she asked, her voice trembling.

The Glory Wind

"It might seem like I never pay much mind to anything, but the truth is, I take things in," Carmella said. "Remember how much you admired my lavender apron? And you told me once that you like springtime best of all the seasons. Made sense to me then, that you'd be partial to a lavender-coloured flower that blooms in spring."

"Oh, I *am*," Gracie said, hugging the pencil box.

The movement made her aware that something had jiggled inside, so she slid the cover open. Inside were three regular pencils, one red one, and a pink eraser.

I opened mine and found the same. When I looked up again, I found Carmella's eyes on me. "Thanks a lot, Carmella," I said. "This is really cool, and I really like the eagle."

"I suppose you're wondering why I picked an eagle," Carmella said. She was right, and I nodded, which prompted her to go on. "School is a blessing, to be sure, but it can also be hard by times, no doubt about it. This is to remind you that I'm lifting up your name to the Good Lord every night before I close my eyes, asking Him to watch and guide and care for you. And Gracie too, of course."

I was wondering what that had to do with an eagle when

Carmella went on. "I picked an eagle for you from one of my favourite passages in the Good Book. From Isaiah, chapter 40, verse 31: 'But they that wait upon the LORD shall renew their strength; they shall mount up with wings as eagles; they shall run, and not be weary; and they shall walk, and not faint.'"

"That's lovely, isn't it Luke?" Ma said.

Lovely isn't a word I would personally use to describe *anything*. "It's great, Carmella," I said. "And thanks for the stuff inside too."

"I had to leave school after grade five, myself," Carmella said. "It just warms my heart to see you children learning. And it's your first time at a new school, Gracie—you must be excited about that. And it's a great place to make new friends too."

"I'll have *lots* of friends," Gracie agreed, "but Luke will be my best friend, right Luke?"

If Gracie had looked at me square on right at that moment, she'd have seen that something was wrong. But she was caught up with the pencil box and Carmella's visit, so she barely glanced in my direction.

I stood there without opening my mouth while my last chance slipped away. And then Carmella spoke.

"My, my! Then things sure have changed since I went to school."

"What do you mean?" Gracie asked. She stopped fiddling with the pencil box.

"Why, just that I never knew of *any* school where the girls and boys play much together, not at your age."

Gracie seemed to be thinking about that. Her face got a kind of pinched look that I'd seen whenever she was pondering hard on something.

"Maybe it's different here, is it Luke?" Carmella asked.

"No, that's how it is all right," I said. I was trying to sound unhappy about it, but inside I was doing handstands and whooping.

"Well, I think that's stupid," Gracie declared.

"Sure it is, but it could be fun too," Carmella said.

"Fun? How?" Gracie demanded.

"Like, if you made a game of it—keeping your friendship a secret when you're around other kids," Carmella said.

"That might be okay," I said. "If it was a game, I mean."

"We could have secret words and signals," Gracie squealed. Her eyes had lit up and were snapping with excitement at the idea.

My relief was so great that I almost missed the small,

satisfied smile on Carmella's face. That was when I realized she'd known, somehow, just what was bothering me and had found a way to fix it. I gave her the hint of a nod and her left eye flashed a wink in reply.

Later that day, Gracie did her best to make me memorize a long and complicated list of words that we were to use in our secret communications. The flaw, which she somehow missed, was that there would be few opportunities to use her code. It hardly mattered anyway, because by the next morning when the school bus arrived, I'd forgotten most of them altogether, and was only half sure about the few that lingered in my brain.

Chapter Ten

It turned out that I really didn't have much to worry about at all. As soon as we got off the bus at school, the girls swept in and claimed Gracie, dragging her off and swarming around her like locusts on a green field. I was a bit alarmed, the way they were crowded in on her, giggling and squealing and hollering to be heard over each other. It looked almost scary as they tugged and competed for her attention. I could hardly see her there in the middle of the cluster, but the few glimpses I got told me Gracie was actually enjoying the attention. She was smiling, her eyes shining and her cheeks as pink as if she'd been running on a cold, windy day.

I was trying to keep an eye on Gracie—just to make sure everything was going all right—and still pay attention to what Pete and Brandon were saying. The three of us had gathered together as automatically as if we'd been at school together the day before, although we'd barely seen each other all summer. Brandon was telling us about a new hired man who'd nearly set fire to their barn one morning.

"It would've burned too, sure as shootin' if it wasn't for me," Brandon said. "The men were gone out to the fields when I went to get a piece of rope and spotted a curl of smoke rising up from some damp hay."

"Were there flames?" Pete wanted to know.

"No, but there'd a-been some in a few more minutes," Brandon told us. "It was just gettin' ready to spark when I happened along and stomped it out. Poured water on it too, to make sure."

It wasn't much of a story, especially for Brandon. He does heroic things pretty regular—you never saw a guy who could run into so many dangerous situations just in the nick of time the way he does. Then I realized he was watching what was going on with the girls too.

"They sure know how to make spectacles of themselves," he said, nodding toward the tittering cluster. "All this fuss over a new girl. Just look at 'em!"

We looked, shaking our heads scornfully and turning disgusted faces to each other. I'd never really paid attention to girls and their goings-on before but this was different. Gracie was at the middle of it and that made me curious.

"I have eighty-seven marbles," Sharon Goldrick announced loudly. "You can come over to my house sometime and play with them, Gracie."

This started a strange sort of competition where the other girls shouted out what kind of toys they had too. Paper dolls and dominos and games like Snakes and Ladders and Finance were offered as lures to get Gracie to visit.

Gracie just kept smiling and saying things like, "That would be nice," until they'd all run out of enticements. That was when they switched from bribery to flattery.

"I just love your hair, Gracie!" Evelyn Hamm gushed. "Are those natural curls?"

"They certainly are," Gracie said. "My daddy just adored them. He was a war hero, but before that he loved to buy me hair ribbons. He bought me every colour he could find. My mother says I have ribbons in every shade of the rainbow!"

An admiring "*ooh*" rose from the group. A couple of the girls even clapped their hands, which caused Brandon to elbow me in the ribs and snicker.

"You're so *lucky* to have natural curls," Millie Vangard said, fluffing her own hair with one hand. "I have to get mine from a Toni Home Perm."

Millie's dry, frizzy hair was nothing to brag about, but she had looked pleased when she made this announcement.

"I *hate* home perms," Dorothy Fleming declared with a huff. "They stink!"

"And they *hurt*," Sharon said. "Least, they do when my Aunt Bernice gives them. She near yanks the hair right out of a person when she's putting in the curling rods. My head was sore for a week last time she gave me one."

"I guess I *am* lucky to have natural curly hair, then," Gracie said, looking down modestly. This drew the girls' attention back to her and brought out a fresh batch of compliments.

Just like that, Gracie stepped into the girls' world as easily as she had walked into mine that day in the field. They took her into their circle, and by all appearances, they were awfully fond of her. For her part, Gracie was every bit as friendly and nice to them as they were to her.

I wondered, by times, how it was that she could be so much like the others, skipping rope and playing hopscotch and tag and such, and yet be so completely different too.

I was glad for her, glad that she had lots of new friends. Gracie shone in the middle of them and, unlike me, she

The Glory Wind

clearly loved being the centre of attention. Why, the first day, when Miss Prutko asked her if she'd like to introduce herself to the class, she marched up to the front and took up half of the first period telling everyone about her daddy being a war hero and her collection of hair ribbons and the long way she and her mom had travelled to move to Junction and all kinds of other things. Then, when she went back to her seat and Miss Prutko told us all to make her feel welcome, everyone clapped like they really meant it.

Everything had worked out perfectly. At school we each had our own friends and paid no mind to each other. But after school and on Saturdays, there were just the two of us, and we were happy with that.

And that's how it all went along—for a very short while.

PART THREE

The Darkening

Not all tornados have funnel clouds. Under certain weather conditions, there's no telltale column whirling through the air, looking for just the right place to touch down. And, of course, when you can't see something coming, it's hard to prepare for it.

Chapter Eleven

Kevin Sarrazin was a nice guy. I suppose a person would have to be, to make a living as a travelling salesman, which is what Kevin did. He travelled from town to town in a '36 Chevy Town Sedan, peddling a wide assortment of wares out of the big black case that he kept stocked from boxes in the car's trunk. If you saw Kevin, you knew that case was somewhere nearby.

Kevin had never been to Junction before that October. It had always been a tall, thin, cigar-puffing man named George Renner. George had been visiting the town with his household products for years, but that summer he'd taken ill with consumption and Kevin was assigned to his territory.

As I said, he was a nice guy. He was young and friendly, with a way about him that folks took to right off. Maybe it was the smooth way he talked, or the fact that his blue eyes were always smiling, but everybody warmed up to Kevin

The Glory Wind

fast. People liked him, plain and simple.

And of course, when you like someone, you don't just look over their wares and buy a useful-looking gadget or two and then send them on their way. You put out tea and lay out a plate of corn bread, and talk about the crops and the weather and, most of all, your neighbours.

And that's exactly what happened at Miss Laird's place. Miss Laird is an old maid who fills her days gathering up what she can of other people's business. It's probably what she has to do to keep herself from being too bored. And I wouldn't care, except that when Kevin Sarrazin called on her with his big black case, she saw a chance to help fill the long day stretching out in front of her. Miss Laird put some pork hocks on to boil, and when she'd finished looking over his fine products, she told him dinner was almost ready—and of course he had to be polite and stay.

That was when the talk swung to Raedine Moor and how she'd come to Junction not long ago. And wouldn't you know it, Kevin knew Raedine from her old town.

I can tell you what he said because I heard it quoted more than once over the next few weeks. The ladies' social ladder rearranged itself the way it does when anyone has big news, and Miss Laird became the most visited woman in Junction. Everyone who'd been there repeated the story.

"He said that he knew the Moors very well, that they had actually lived a few doors away from his family when Raedine was young. Miss Laird said that those were his *exact words*!"

The end of the story always came with a head nod and a properly shocked expression, although a few couldn't quite hide their pleasure at the telling.

I was puzzled at first. I couldn't find the scandal in the remark. Then Patty Dempsey, Keane's fifteen-year-old sister, made a point of coming up to me in the playground at school and clearing it up.

"You might just as well know, Luke Haliwell, that you won't be welcome at our house anymore so long as you're prancing about the fields with that horrid *Moor* girl," she told me. "Her mother is a liar and a harlot."

I was nowhere near sure what a *harlot* was, so I focused on the other half of her statement and asked, "What did she lie about?"

"Why, about being a widow, of course. She was born and raised Raedine *Moor*. She never had a husband at all—which means Gracie never had a father. No decent person will want to be around them ever again. My mother even said so."

The Glory Wind

As she talked, my thoughts moved from what she was saying, to her face, which had gotten closer and closer to mine as she spoke. Red blotches lit up her cheeks and spittle formed at the corners of her mouth.

I wanted to punch her—to knock her teeth right down her throat. At the very least, I wanted to call her names that would mean a strapping when she told, and she *would* tell. But something inside me was frozen in fascination at the ugliness in her face, the way it was twisted with a sort of gloating hate, and the sound of her words—the meanness in them, and the spite.

I managed to move at last, but it wasn't to strike anyone. My body followed my head in a slow turn as my eyes searched the faces on the playground, looking for Gracie.

She was standing not ten feet away. She was very still, her eyes fixed on Patty, her face expressionless. There was no doubt that she'd heard everything.

The playground's natural sounds were dying off as a widening circle of students sensed something happening and turned their attention toward it. Gracie took a step toward Patty and then another. Her hands were tiny balls at her side.

"My daddy was a war hero," she said softly.

"You don't even *have* a daddy, you liar," Patty said with a sneer.

"My daddy died fighting for his country," Gracie said, a little louder.

"I *said* you don't *have* a daddy!"

The colour was coming back to Gracie's face, which had been ghostly a moment before. She crossed her arms in what seemed a brave and defiant act to me at the time.

"I do so have a daddy!" she shouted. Her eyes shifted and found me. "Tell her Luke!"

I was fighting my way past the dryness of my throat, trying to find the words and the courage to say them, when Patty spoke again.

"What does Luke know?" she asked scornfully. "Luke's own daddy..."

"SHUT UP!" I screamed. "Just shut up, shut up, shut up! You don't know anything, Patty Dempsey. *You're* the liar! A big, stupid liar."

My outburst brought Miss Prutko, her arms waving as she called, "Stop! Stop this right now! *What* is going on here?"

"Luke yelled and called me names," Patty reported at once. "*I* wasn't doing anything."

The Glory Wind

"Luke?" Miss Prutko's eyes found me. "What do you have to say for yourself?"

I couldn't defend myself, not without repeating what Patty had said about Gracie. I shrugged and said nothing, even though I really liked Miss Prutko and I hated the idea of her having a low opinion of me.

She told me to go inside and wait at my desk, where she joined me moments later.

Standing beside the desk I shared with John Younger, she asked me for a second time if I had anything to say.

"No, ma'am."

"I can't see you behaving this way for no reason," she prodded.

I remained silent, staring ahead. An odd pain throbbed in my chest and I had the uncomfortable feeling that if I looked at Miss Prutko I was going to disgrace myself and cry.

She stood there, waiting. I suppose she imagined that I'd crack if she let a few moments pass, but in fact the effect on me was quite the opposite. As seconds went by, the urge to shout out my defence passed, and in no time my mind was made up that nothing would induce me to speak.

"Then I have no choice but to punish you, Luke," Miss

Prutko said at last. "Come with me."

I followed her to the front of the classroom and stood, teeth clenched, while she lifted down the strap. It felt as though my heart might pound its way right out of my chest as I stood there, waiting.

"Hold out your right hand."

I made a confused false start with my left, realized my mistake, and thrust the correct hand forward. Miss Prutko lifted the strap up and brought it down, and it really didn't hurt very much. But the crack of the leather against my hand startled me and I made a sort of "*unh!*" sound while she gave me two more cracks. The ache in my chest had grown but it had nothing to do with the strap hurting.

Miss Prutko hesitated before saying softly, "Now the other one."

I lifted my left hand and took the blows without reacting at all.

"Take your seat, Luke," Miss Prutko said. She went then to the front wall and tugged at the rope, ringing the bell to call the others in from recess.

They spilled and crowded through the doorway, their excited chatter dying down as they plunked into their seats. A few glanced at me but it seemed most of them had already forgotten the scene outside.

Not Gracie, of course. I felt her eyes on me all afternoon, and at the end of the day, when the bus delivered us to our stop, she made a sort of speech, which I could tell she'd been rehearsing in her head.

"I saw it all through the window, Luke. I know you took a strapping, and I know why," she told me. "You could have got out of it if you'd told Miss Prutko what happened. And I know why you didn't: so you wouldn't have to repeat those—those horrid *lies* to her."

She reached out then, and took my hand. "Thank you, Luke."

"Forget it," I said, red-faced. The only thing I wanted to do was get out of there so I wouldn't have to look at her shining, grateful eyes.

I'd have rather taken a hundred strappings than feel the way I did right then—with her thanking me for something I didn't even do. I'd wanted to stand up for her all right, but the truth was I hadn't opened my mouth until Patty Dempsey brought up *my* father.

There was no way I could tell Gracie I'd actually been protecting myself.

Chapter Twelve

My father isn't a coward—I want to state that right off. I've seen him stand up to much bigger men on those occasions when one of the farmhands we hire at harvest gets a little drink in him and turns mean. And one year, when there was a fire in the barn, he went in there six times to get the horses out, even though there were burning chunks of wood falling and the smoke was thick enough to cut.

These are things I've seen for myself. It's harder to explain something you haven't seen, something you've only heard about. All you have then are other people's ideas and memories and words. You can't trust any of that the same way you can trust your own eyes and ears.

We were at war from the time I was a little kid and I accepted it like I did any other normal part of my life. I guess that was because it went back to all of my earliest memories—talk of

The Glory Wind

the war threading its way through so many conversations.

I hadn't thought much about why some men were gone off to fight while others were still around. Others like my father.

That changed at our yearly Sunday School picnic the year I was eight. The picnic was something that created as much excitement in Junction as a carnival would in bigger places. We had pony rides and relay races and a scavenger hunt, and games like Simon Says and ring toss and hot potato. There were games for the adults too: tug-of-war and horseshoes—mostly for the men. And, of course, there were all sorts of good things to eat.

I won a bright blue yo-yo for being the last one out at hot potato, and that was when the trouble started. Terry Stafford decided he wanted that yo-yo.

Terry was a couple of years older and a whole lot bigger than me. He came over and stood almost nose-to-nose and gave me an imitation of a smile.

"Hey! Want to trade?" he asked, offering me a paperback book of some sort. It already had a crease bent in the cover, no doubt from his careless handling.

"Nope."

"Why not?"

"I just don't." I slipped the loop of string over my finger

and clenched the yo-yo in my hand. I'd seen Terry make "trades" before.

He looked angry. I could see it growing in him, could see him thinking, deciding what to do next. I took a quick glance toward the group of women, where my mother was. They were laughing and talking as they organized the food for lunch. My ma was chatting with the others, oblivious to the problem that was starting up for me.

I willed her to look my way, but she didn't. She would have heard me if I'd called to her, but that was out of the question. It's one thing if your mother comes along and butts in on something and takes up for you on her own. You can act like you're embarrassed and put out over it, even if you're secretly relieved. You'll get ribbed and called a momma's boy, but as long as everyone saw it wasn't your fault, that will hardly last out the day. It's another story altogether if you *ask* your mother to help. The brand you'd get for *that* could last for years.

So I stayed quiet and waited. I didn't have to wait long, because Terry took a step forward, pulling my full attention back to him. His jaw was thrust out a little and there was an angry blaze in his eyes.

"Luke thinks he's some kind of hot shot because he

has a stupid yo-yo," he said, turning to the kids who were standing around, waiting for the next game to begin.

"Do not," I said. I hated the way my voice sounded shaky and small.

The slap came so suddenly that I had no time to defend myself. It stung my cheek and sent me reeling backwards. I half stumbled but caught myself and stayed on my feet.

"I guess he's like his father," Terry said. "Acts big and all, when he's really nothing but a yellow-bellied coward."

"My father is *not* a coward!" I cried.

"Oh, no? So, how come he's not over there fighting in the war like most of the men from these parts?"

"He couldn't go," I said. "He got hurt."

Terry forced out a short, sharp laugh. "He got hurt," he repeated. He shook his head like he'd never heard anything quite so funny. "That's a real laugh, boy."

"He *did* get hurt," I insisted.

"You think anybody around here believes *that*?" Terry snorted. "Your daddy busted up his own leg on purpose, the day before he was supposed to ship out. He did it because he wasn't man enough to go and fight."

I lunged at him, fists flying. Fury blurred my vision as I swung wildly, calling him a dirty liar and demanding that he take it back.

Of course, as soon as I'd lost the advantage of surprise, Terry's superior weight and strength took over. He slammed his fist into my midsection with enough force to drive me to the ground. I landed on my back with a thud that I could actually hear, and that drove the breath from me. I was still too angry to think rationally, so I gulped in some air and yelled a few more insults. He kicked me in the side a couple of times and might have gone on kicking, except the women had rushed over and pulled him away.

His mother caught him as he lurched unsteadily, off balance from being yanked back. She was a tall, thin woman with a pointed face and tight, thin lips. Taking hold of Terry's ear, she yelled, "What do you mean by picking on a kid half your size? You oughta be ashamed of yourself! Now, you apologize to Luke—and his mother too!"

"He came at *me*," Terry grumbled, forgetting that he'd slapped me first. He tugged and rubbed at his ear sullenly. "I never hit him at the start."

"He said my father hurt himself on purpose because he was scared to fight in the war!" I shouted as the women turned to look at me.

The silence was instant, like a switch had been thrown

to turn off the sound. It was my mother who broke it.

"I wonder where your boy might have heard such a thing," she said in a calm, quiet voice. She didn't seem shocked at all by what I'd just said.

"Now, Alice, surely you don't think...that I..." Mrs. Stafford started, but then it was like she ran out of words because her mouth kept moving with nothing coming out.

"Of course not," Ma said smoothly. "I wouldn't dream of making an accusation unless I knew all the facts. Unless I knew them for certain."

Then it seemed that no one was looking at me or Ma, or even each other. I was on my feet again and Ma had me pulled against her, facing out, like I was a shield of some sort, though I don't think that was her intention. Her hands had settled on my shoulders in a firm grasp but she needn't have worried about me trying to get away. My sides and stomach were both aching from the blows they'd received, and I was perfectly content to lean against my mother and know I was safe.

I stayed there while she stood them down, waiting until they'd all turned and begun to shuffle off. Not one of them had a thing to say.

I asked my ma about it later, when we were back home.

Exactly what had happened to my father's leg. I knew he walked with a limp, but it had always been there in my recollection and I'd never thought to wonder about it.

"Folks around here just love to talk," she said after a bit of a pause. "I suppose it looked bad, his injury coming right at that time, but people will talk no matter when a thing happens. They need to point fingers and judge others so they don't have to look too close at themselves."

"But he *didn't* do it on purpose like Terry said, right Ma?"

"I don't believe a man's honour should need defending in his own home, do you?" she said. "Now, not another word about it."

I managed to stay cross at my ma for the next few weeks for not telling me out-and-out that it wasn't true. I'm sure she felt my anger running just under the surface, making me pull back ever so slightly when she combed my hair or touched me for any reason. But she bore it without comment or question while it worked its way through and out of me.

It was years before it occurred to me that my father really was the only person in the whole world who knew the truth for sure.

Chapter Thirteen

The shunning of Gracie began almost immediately after that day in the school playground. At first, it was like she had become invisible, for all the mind anyone paid to her. For the rest of that week, the other girls walked right past her with their heads lifted, careful not to let their eyes drift toward her.

It was strangely fascinating to watch friendships shift and move, rearranging themselves as seamlessly as if Gracie had never been included among them. The circle that had opened and taken her in, pushed her out and closed behind her just as efficiently. Instead of new friends, Gracie was surrounded by empty space.

It got worse the next week.

Gracie had been sharing a double desk with Ursula Bjarki, a dull, square-faced girl with a habit of chewing on the tips of her braided hair.

But on Monday of the week after the stories started, when Gracie reached the desk, she found a stack of books piled where she would normally sit. She asked Ursula to please move them. Ursula gave her a haughty look.

"My mother doesn't want me to sit next to you," Ursula said with obvious satisfaction.

"But where will I sit then?" Gracie asked. She seemed less concerned with the snub than with the matter of where she was to do her work. "There aren't any extra places."

She remained there for the next few moments, until Miss Prutko came along and told her to sit down.

"I can't, ma'am. Ursula's mother doesn't want me to sit with her anymore, and there are no empty seats."

"My mother sent a note for you, Miss Prutko," Ursula said at once. "She said she was sure you'd understand perfectly well why I shouldn't have to sit by a—"

"Where is this note?" Miss Prutko asked before Ursula could finish. She frowned as she unfolded and read the square of paper Ursula produced. After a slight pause, she instructed Sharon Goldrick to go and sit with Ursula, and Gracie was sent to join Mira Anderson in Sharon's vacated spot.

The next morning, *Mira* had a note from her mother. Gracie was moved a second time and she remained at that desk until Friday, when yet another note was produced.

Through this shuffling of seats, Gracie seemed to be unaffected by the snubs and letters and rejections. She took each slight with so little reaction that you'd have thought her wholly indifferent.

I knew the truth.

"Can you believe it, Luke? They were all my friends before, and now they're so horrid! It's like they hate me, but I haven't *done* anything!" The comment burst from her as though it had been building all day. We'd just gotten off the bus—it was on Friday, after the third time a parent's note had forced Miss Prutko to move Gracie.

"I don't think they hate you...not really," I said. I searched my head for something else to tell her, but just then Gracie tossed her head.

"Anyway, why should I care if they do?" she declared. "I don't care, that's what!"

That let me off the hook, which was a relief since I had no idea what else I was supposed to say. I thought she might bring it up again, but the weekend passed without a mention.

And then it was Monday, and we arrived at school to find something new in the classroom. It was a desk, not unlike the others but made for one person instead of two, and while our desks were plain wood, it was painted white. In place of the benches we all sat on, there was a matching white chair with a small pink cushion on it.

The girls gathered around it with little admiring comments, each of them pretending to hope it was for a friend. Anyone could see that every last one of them was really longing for it for herself.

Only Gracie made no move toward it, although I saw her glancing at it from the side of the room. She was to sit with Evelyn Hamm that morning, but Evelyn had warned her on their way in that she needn't bother trying to take the seat.

I took in the scene around me—the girls giggling and chattering, Gracie standing alone by the wall—and a strange feeling grew in my chest. I wanted that desk to be for Gracie—wanted it more than I'd ever wanted anything before. It came over me so powerfully I could hardly keep from shouting that the desk *must* be for Gracie.

Another moment and it might have burst out of me, but thankfully, Miss Prutko had finished what she was doing at the board, and she turned and looked about the room until her eyes rested on Gracie.

The Glory Wind

"Gracie," Miss Prutko said, pointing to the new white desk and chair. "This will be your desk for the rest of the year."

Of course, a murmur of protest rippled over the girls' side of the room at once. Shocked and angry whispers rose but were quickly quashed when Miss Prutko said, quite sharply, "Class!"

I could have laughed with joy as Gracie made her way to the desk, her eyes shining. She leaned over and pressed her hand into the pink cushion and then watched it rise back into shape before she turned slightly and settled herself onto it.

"Why should *she* get to sit there?" mumbled Mira, unable to contain her outrage.

"Was there something you wanted to say, Mira?" Miss Prutko asked. Her voice was calm and quiet, but there was a dangerous undertone in it, and Mira was wise enough to hold her tongue after that.

I know Miss Prutko was just trying to stand up for Gracie. She prettied up the desk and chair as a way to make up for the cruel way the other girls had been treating her. She could have left them plain and nothing would have come of it. In fact, it might have been a *good* thing. Gracie would have had somewhere to sit and no one could have kicked up any sort of fuss about not wanting to be next to her.

I wonder sometimes, if she had to do it all over again, whether Miss Prutko would have painted that desk and chair. That was what caused all the trouble—something as simple as a coat of white paint and a little pink cushion.

Chapter Fourteen

In telling this, I'm surprised to find that I'm still learning things about the truth. I started to tell you how Gracie's belief that I had stood up to Patty Dempsey on her account had worked on my conscience and nudged me to do the right thing. But I can see that I was giving myself more credit than I deserved.

Not that my conscience, nagging away at me, didn't have a lot to do with it, but I can now see that Miss Prutko played a big part too. It was her example that gave me the last push I needed.

Things were getting worse for Gracie with each day that passed. The classroom was bad enough, but the playground was worse. Miss Prutko's presence kept things under control inside, but once we were in the yard, there wasn't a lot of supervision. She checked on us, but only now and then, and not nearly enough to prevent the meanness that just kept growing.

Most of it was words, and believe me, there were plenty of those. A lot of kids walked straight up to Gracie and said things right to her face. Mean things. It wasn't like she was bothering anybody or giving them any reason to act that way, but they didn't seem to need a reason.

"*You* have no father, Gracie Moor!"

"You're a liar, Gracie Moor!"

They called her things like "dirty" and "smelly" and told her to get away from them, even though *they* had approached *her*.

I don't know which was worse, the words they shouted into her face or the ones that were delivered in loud whispers. You knew when it was coming, the way their eyes followed her to watch her reaction—to make sure she heard the things they said behind their hands.

Perhaps the cruelest of all were the mocking imitations of Gracie. "*My* daddy *loved* my curly hair! Oh, wait! I just remembered—I don't *have* a daddy!"

It took Miss Prutko and the white desk to make me cross the line. I'd been sitting in class that morning, watching Gracie at her desk, her small shoulders hunched over her work. I noticed that she wasn't pushing her hair back, as was her habit—tossing it over her shoulder or tucking it behind her ear.

That morning, her hair had fallen down around her face but she had just left it there. All of a sudden, I knew that Gracie was hiding, protecting herself the best way she could from the stares and sniggers around her.

Something about her bowed head and hunched shoulders forced me to look away.

But at lunchtime, after our paper bags had been folded and returned to our knapsacks and we'd all made our way back to the yard, I could feel her aloneness as she stood by herself and waited for the noon break to be over with. It was like an invisible line had been drawn around Gracie and no one could go past it.

I found myself crossing to where she stood.

She looked up at me, surprised and a little fearful. Her face didn't relax until I offered a weak smile. Even then, it remained solemn.

"You'd better think real hard about this, Luke," she said in a low voice. "You know what will happen, don't you?"

I did know, and I *had* thought about it. In fact, I'd been thinking about it since the first day Gracie had to move seats. I'd thought about it when I was doing my chores after school, or eating supper, or lying in bed at night. I hadn't been able to get away from thinking about it.

So when Gracie asked me if I knew what I was getting myself into, I nodded and squared my shoulders the way I'd seen Pa do when he was about to take care of something he didn't much care to do, like put down a lame horse.

Gracie gave me a long, careful look. It reminded me of the way she'd stared at a dead butterfly we'd found one August morning. Her eyes had swept over it with a slow, searching sadness, as though she might be able to see what had caused its death if she looked hard enough.

Gracie wasn't the only one looking. I felt the stares that went with the ripple of whispers behind me. At that moment, I didn't care. The only fear in me was that I might care later on, and this wasn't something I could ever undo.

It turned out that the boys weren't nearly as good at shunning a person as the girls were. The fellows my age made some snide comments all right, and they made a general sort of effort to ignore me, but you could see their hearts weren't in it. Not like the girls.

The girls, of course, did ignore me, but it was impossible for me to see that as a bad thing.

Chapter Fifteen

When she'd been working at the Prairie Inn for about a month, Raedine started to come home late one or two evenings a week. She'd land at the door to get Gracie with a breathless explanation that she'd had to work past her normal shift. Ma said she was happy to have a chance to show some Christian kindness, even in the summertime when Gracie had been around all day. We would just set an extra plate at dinner and, if Raedine was really late, Gracie would be put to sleep on the daybed until her mother finally arrived.

But after the stories about Raedine never having been married started to go around, Ma's Christian kindness wasn't quite as conspicuous. I heard her talking about the situation with Pa one evening when they thought I was asleep.

I'm not sure how long the conversation had been going on, but it came through more and more clearly as their voices rose. I guess I started to hear whole sentences around the time Ma said, "To think that I defended the woman! It's not that I'm *judging* Raedine, Jack. People make mistakes. It's the way she lied to us and made fools of us."

"I don't suppose she thought she had much of a choice," Pa said in a neutral voice.

"You *would* take her part!"

"Now hold on right there, Alice. I'm not taking anyone's part. I'm just saying, you can't punish the little one for something that's not her fault."

"Who's talking about punishing her? I just don't know that I want to be doing her mother any more favours, is all."

"Then I guess the child can stay by herself until her mother gets home from work from now on. That's what will happen if she can't come here and you know it. Raedine isn't going to find anyone else who'll watch Gracie now. Not after those busybodies have been hard at work."

There was silence for a bit, then the sound of a newspaper being snapped open. I could picture Pa picking it up and reading, while Ma sat with her knitting and gave it some more thought. Ma could think on an argument for days and then suddenly bring it back up when Pa thought for sure he'd heard the last of it.

The Glory Wind

I was nervous because she was thinking about not letting Gracie come over any more while Raedine was at work, even though I didn't think she'd really do it. She liked Gracie, and besides that she was always saying how nice it was for me to have a friend to play with, and how much less she worried about me now. But you never knew for sure with Ma. In any case, I wanted to know how it came out, so I slid out of bed and crept to the top of the stairs so I wouldn't miss anything. I was glad to hear Ma start into it again a half hour later.

"I suppose you're right about it not being Gracie's fault," she said. The paper rustled as Pa lowered it, something Ma insisted on when they were talking.

"Uh, huh?" he said.

"So, I guess she can keep coming here. It's nice for Luke to have a friend anyway. But there are two things I won't allow, and I expect you to back me up on both of them.

"Except for the few moments it takes for her to pick up her daughter, Raedine Moor will never be welcomed into this house again. And Luke is not to go to her house anymore, for any reason."

"I see. Well, that seems reasonable, all right. How do you mean to explain it to Luke?"

She didn't answer right away, so I guess she hadn't thought that far ahead. When she did speak, it was with a heavy sigh. "That's one of the problems in this kind of situation. I don't want Luke being exposed to talk of such things. But you're right—I'll need to think of something to tell him."

The explanation she came up with the next morning when she told me I wasn't to go to the Moors' house anymore was, "because I'm your mother and I said so." She needn't have worried. I was so relieved at the outcome that I would never have asked.

Chapter Sixteen

Mayor Anstruther called a town meeting just a few weeks later. It seemed that everyone in Junction was there, and Ma and Pa were no exception. It happened to be one of the nights Raedine was late coming for Gracie, which was how it came to be that Gracie and I were there too.

If I'd been home by myself, I could have stayed alone. But since Gracie was still there, Ma insisted that we go along. She said she was responsible for watching Gracie and there was no way she was leaving her.

When we got to the Junction Town Hall, it was decided that Gracie and I were to wait in the back of the truck while my folks went into the meeting. Pa predicted that it wouldn't last more than half an hour at the most, an opinion Ma didn't share, judging by the look she gave him. We were strictly warned not to go anywhere near the building. Apparently, this was not a matter for children to concern themselves with.

They might as well have told us to get as close as possible. We waited only until cars and trucks had stopped arriving and everyone had gone inside. Then, we crept over to the side of the hall and crouched under a window near the platform end of the room, hoping to hear enough to find out what was going on.

The first ten minutes or so were taken up by Mayor Anstruther talking, his voice rising and falling in a rhythm I'd heard before at public gatherings. It was neither loud nor clear enough for us to make out any actual words, and we had a whispered exchange about going back to the truck, where we could at least move around and talk out loud.

We were on the verge of leaving when a scraping sound right over our heads made us freeze in place, hearts pounding at the thought of discovery. As we sat, as still as stones, the sound was repeated several more times, although not as nearby.

It only took us a few seconds to realize the sound had been that of windows being pulled open—beginning with the one right above us. Almost immediately we heard "that's much better," and "a body can hardly breathe in this crowd," and such.

We'd just been given access to everything that was going on inside, and we could hardly suppress our glee. It was as if one of the secret missions we dreamed up in the Circle of Truth and carried out skulking around the fields, spying on farmers, had turned into a sort of reality. We'd been forbidden to listen, and yet there we were, about to take it all in.

The mayor was wrapping up by then, ending with a little campaigning as he finished his spiel. Then he said he was calling on Alvin Dempsey, who would speak on behalf of a newly formed Citizens' Committee. Mr. Dempsey must have been close to the front, because his voice boomed out a second later.

"I guess we all know why we're here tonight. A situation has developed at the school, and it needs righting at once."

As soon as I heard him mention the school I knew we shouldn't be there, under that window, listening. I knew my pa had been right, and whatever was going to be said wasn't something we ought to be hearing.

I said as much to Gracie but she wasn't buying it. Like me, she'd understood immediately that they were all gathered there to talk about the painted desk.

Valerie Sherrard

And so we stayed and listened. The way they were talking, you'd have thought that Miss Prutko had put Gracie on a golden throne and demanded that the other girls curtsey to her when they went by.

Mr. Dempsey's speech went on and on. He said that it was outrageous and appalling that someone in a teacher's position, someone who had been entrusted to set a proper example for her class, could have made such a complete mockery of common decency. It was truly beyond the committee's comprehension and they would not, *could* not, tolerate it for one second longer.

Come what may, Gracie Moor was not to sit at the painted desk ever again.

Beside me in the growing dark, Gracie offered a small shrug.

"The Chair recognizes Leah Zecchino."

A surprised murmur ran through the crowd at this announcement. Everyone knew Leah was shy and quiet— probably the last person they might have expected to ask for the floor in a meeting.

By this time it had grown dark enough outside for us to risk peeking in at the corner of the window, so we watched as the pretty young woman made her way forward, turned, and faced the gathered crowd.

"Hello," she began, her voice trembling. "I guess you all know me since I grew up hereabouts. And you know I'm not a person who usually has much to say."

Nods and murmurs of assent ran through the room.

"So I imagine you're surprised to see me standing here and you're probably wondering what could make me want to get up in front of a roomful of people.

"Like I said, I grew up here, and I went to that very school where Miss Prutko is teaching this year. I went there and so did my brothers...and my cousins."

There was a pause during which Leah slowly scanned the crowd. "I guess most of you remember my cousin Eliza and her family, even though they moved east going on ten years ago."

People were starting to look at the floor. Leah took a tiny step forward, her face pale and earnest. "My cousin Eliza Price sat in that schoolhouse every day from grade one to five. She sat there with her cleft palate and a tongue that didn't quite stay in her mouth. She wasn't so pretty to look at—but she didn't ask to be born that way, did she?

"For five years Eliza was made fun of by the other children and no one did one single thing about it. It was as though it was all right to treat her unkindly because she had that deformity. That was her childhood from the time she was six until she was eleven. Sitting in that schoolhouse, taking in all the meanness and hurt...until the day of the tragedy. You all know what happened. And then she never sat in that classroom again.

"This business about the desk has had me thinking about Eliza for the past while. Eliza didn't ask to be born with a cleft palate any more than Gracie Moor asked to be born in her situation. I can't help thinking that maybe if someone had shown my cousin some kindness, the way Miss Prutko is doing with Gracie, then things might have turned out differently for Eliza too.

"So I'm standing up here to ask you to remember Eliza... and to look in your hearts. Please don't make another little girl feel like an outcast when she hasn't done anything to deserve it. And that's all I have to say."

We watched as Leah made her way to the back of the room and sat down.

"What happened to Eliza?" Gracie whispered.

I shrugged. "I dunno. I never heard of her before."

Leah Zecchino's brave speech had changed the feeling in the room. Even from outside the window we could feel the anger and meanness lifting. For a few moments it seemed that maybe everything was going to be all right. And then Alvin Dempsey was on his feet again, his face flushed.

"What about *our* girls and the way *they're* being made feel, to see this, this *other girl* treated better than the rest of them, and her coming from such a low situation? Is this Moor creature to be raised above our own daughters?"

And from there, it was only a matter of a few moments before the crowd's opinion had shifted back. Only this time, they were talking as if they only cared about doing what was fair to *all* the girls, and even the people who'd been on Gracie's side at the start couldn't find anything to argue about.

A motion was made and passed that Miss Prutko would be told there was to be no further favouritism shown to Gracie, and that all the girls should be given a fair turn at sitting in the special desk. After a little more talk, they also decided that Gracie's turn had been long enough already, and so she wasn't to be allowed to sit at the special desk again for the rest of the school year.

It wasn't until then that I realized Miss Prutko hadn't been at the meeting. I wondered why, since it was all about something she'd done. And somehow, I knew she hadn't been invited.

Chapter Seventeen

Gracie was subdued on the drive home that night, but the next morning when she joined me at the bus stop the spark was back.

"They'll all know, won't they?" Before I could answer, she turned to face me, her eyes blazing. "I bet they can hardly wait to see me get kicked out of that seat. Well, they're not going to see it."

I wondered how she meant to avoid it, but when the bell rang I saw that her plan was simple. She just stood and waited at the back of the room until Miss Prutko looked up from her desk. She seemed surprised to find Gracie there.

"Take your seat, please, Gracie," she said, nodding toward the painted desk.

Gracie made her way there warily, taking slow, uncertain steps. I think she was expecting Miss Prutko to realize her mistake at any second and tell her to stop.

The Glory Wind

An indignant buzz rose from the other girls and I knew Gracie had been right—they'd all heard about the outcome of the meeting.

"What's all the noise about?" Miss Prutko asked. No one answered.

At recess, skipping ropes and hopscotch squares were ignored while the schoolyard buzzed with the indignation of the other girls. Before long, they'd decided among themselves that the newly formed Citizens' Committee must not have been able to reach Miss Prutko the night before. Everyone was absolutely certain that the new rules would be put in place the next day. But the next day came, and the day after, and still Gracie sat at the special desk.

The rest of the week went by. By the following Tuesday, Gracie and I had decided that somehow it had all blown over. We thought that perhaps Miss Prutko had changed the committee's mind.

But on the following Monday when we arrived at school, Miss Prutko wasn't there. Instead, the former schoolmistress, Mrs. Drillon, was at the front of the classroom. She had been the teacher before Miss Prutko, and some of the students had heard unpleasant stories about her from their older siblings.

Mrs. Drillon's harsh voice instructed us to take our seats and be quiet, a dual command we lost no time in obeying. I watched Gracie slide into her place, and I could see by the way her shoulders were slumped and her eyes were downcast that she was expecting what came next.

"Gracie Moor," Mrs. Drillon called. "Remove your books from that desk and go stand at the back of the room. Evelyn Hamm, you will move your things to the desk Gracie was occupying."

Evelyn made her way to the white desk, smirking at Gracie on the way. Gracie continued to stand at the back of the room, holding her books, while Mrs. Drillon told us that Miss Prutko had quit her job and would not be returning.

"I will be filling in until a suitable replacement can be found," she told us, "and I run a tight ship, make no mistake about it!" She then launched into the day's lessons, barking out assignments and assuring us we were all lazy and dull-witted when we didn't keep up to the speed she demanded.

"It seems you've been taught *nothing* in either lessons or conduct," she told us at one point. "Well, I'll soon have things back in shape, you can depend on it."

The Glory Wind

Even though Mrs. Drillon had moved Evelyn to the special desk, it seemed that she had somehow forgotten all about Gracie, who remained standing silently through the first half of the morning. But when recess came Gracie turned toward the door and Mrs. Drillon stopped her at once.

"Miss Moor! You were not told to leave. You will stay right there until you're told otherwise."

Except for lunchtime, when she grudgingly allowed Gracie to eat her sandwich and go to the outhouse, Mrs. Drillon had her stand at the back of the room for the entire day. I tried to send her encouraging looks until Mrs. Drillon's sharp eye caught me.

"Luke Haliwell." The tone of her voice as she said my name sent a chill through me.

"Yes, ma'am?"

"I believe we're all aware that you and Gracie Moor are *special friends*." Titters of nervous laughter started up and died down almost instantly as a yardstick slapped against the desk. "I suppose that her mother is *special friends* with your mother, too—or perhaps with your *father*?"

More snickers broke out at this but were quickly brought in check.

"Be that as it may, I will *not*, do you understand me, *not* tolerate inattentiveness in my classroom. Is that clear?"

"Yes, ma'am."

"Good. Now, come here. I have something that will help you remember." As she said this, she stepped back and lifted the strap from its hanging place.

My only previous experience with the strap had been that single time over the argument with Patty Dempsey. As I stood with my hand out, facing Mrs. Drillon, I reminded myself that it hadn't hurt very much at all. Even though it was embarrassing I stepped forward without any real sense of dread.

The shock of the first whack forced a cry from me. The pain was horrible and my hand instantly felt as though it was on fire. Without thinking, I pulled it away. I cringed as she shouted, "PUT YOUR HAND BACK OUT!"

Trembling, I lifted my hand again. I told myself I would stand it better this time, but the second strike was just as forceful, and it had the advantage of connecting with flesh that was already throbbing. Another involuntary gasp of pain betrayed me.

I took four straps on each hand that day and I'm ashamed to say that by the time it was over I was bawling, even though I could see that this added to the miserable creature's satisfaction.

I prayed that night for harm to befall her, for some injury to strike that would keep her from the class. Later, overcome by guilt, I took it back and told myself that she wouldn't be teaching us for more than a few days.

The next morning there was general dismay when the other girls discovered that their victory had been snatched away—the painted desk was gone. It would be some time before we learned its fate. In its place stood a plain, rough table and a three-legged stool. I saw at once that this would become Gracie's place, and I was right. The seat was quickly dubbed "the milking stool" and Gracie was treated to witless remarks about cows and milk buckets on a regular basis.

Weeks passed and still there was no sign of another teacher coming. Instead, there was the steady stream of cruelty and ridicule that Mrs. Drillon seemed to enjoy heaping on us. Both Gracie and I found ourselves on the receiving end of the strap more than once, and for the flimsiest of reasons. Seeing Gracie stand there and take the pain of that leather strap was worse than getting it myself.

It wasn't long before I overcame my earlier guilt and began to pray in earnest for Mrs. Drillon to be struck dead.

I've heard folks say that children don't understand what death is. It's possible that this is true for children who grow up in the cities, but those of us who live on farms make death's acquaintance at a very early age. I surely knew what it was, and I knew exactly what I was asking for in my anger and hatred toward the woman who was causing both Gracie and me such torment.

I confided in Gracie one day, telling her of my horrible prayers. Rather than being shocked, she was quite interested.

"Will it work?" she asked, her keen eyes watching my face for any sign that I was having her on.

"I don't think so, since it's a bad prayer," I admitted.

"How does this prayer thing actually go then?" she asked.

"Well, since God is good, you have to ask for good things, like for sick people to get better or for other good things to happen."

"And do the sick people always get better?"

"They only get better if it's God's will," I said, reciting the explanation my mother had given to me when Uncle Malcolm died.

"So, God only answers prayers for things He was already

going to do anyway?"

"I'm not sure," I said, feeling suddenly confused.

"Well, anyway, why don't you pray for a new teacher to come? That would be giving someone a job—which is a good thing. And we'd be rid of that awful Mrs. Drillon at the same time."

I agreed that this might be a better plan and changed my petition that night at bedtime, even though in my heart I still hoped something dreadful would happen to Mrs. Drillon.

I can't say whether my altered prayer had anything to do with it or not, but the very next morning when we entered the classroom a new teacher was waiting for us.

Chapter Eighteen

It was a relief to discover that our new teacher, Mr. Wolnoth, wasn't mean. He wasn't much of anything, really. Tall and thin, he taught our lessons with a defeated air, as though he knew in advance that we were unlikely to absorb the information he was offering.

He spent a good deal of time standing in the doorway, smoking and staring off into the distance. Often, when he turned back to face us, it was with a tiny start, as though he was surprised to find himself confronted by a room full of students and didn't know quite what to make of it.

Speculation about him was high for several weeks after he first arrived, but the whispers and gossip settled when it seemed there was nothing very exciting to be learned. He was boarding at the home of one of the older students and she reported that he'd come from Winnipeg in answer to the job posting.

The Glory Wind

"He's never been married and when he's not taking walks, he's mostly in his room," she told us. "The only time we see him is at meals and even then he's as quiet as a church mouse. Why, I think he'd starve if we didn't pass things to him, for he never asks for anything. He's just about the dullest person I ever met."

Gracie had another take on him.

"He seems so sad," she said as we sat together on my back step one Saturday, late in the fall.

"I guess," I said.

"Or maybe it's not sad, exactly. It's more like he's, I don't know...*disappointed* most of the time, don't you think?"

"Disappointed about what?"

This brought an eye-roll and a look of exasperation, but then she laughed, as she often did when she'd decided there was no hope for me to *ever* understand *anything*.

"Never mind," she said, patting my hand. "Let's go to my place for a while."

"Isn't your mom working?" I had never told Gracie that I wasn't supposed to go to her house. Instead, I'd avoided it as much as I could without making her suspicious, and when that wasn't possible I went ahead and hoped I wouldn't get caught. I figured if Ma found out, I could always claim I'd forgotten—at least the first time.

"She was supposed to but she was sick this morning, so she's taking a day off."

"Won't she get in trouble with her boss for not showing up?"

"No. Mr. Manby went to tell him."

"Who?"

"Mr. Manby. He's a new friend of hers. He came over early this morning for breakfast. My mother sent him to tell her boss she was sick but he came right back. His car has a rumble seat; want to go see it?"

"Sure!" Sporty cars were in short supply in Junction, where far more practical means of transportation were the norm. I'd seen coupes before, but never close up.

My eyes could hardly take in the sight of the car that was filling the Moors' gateway when we got there. It was cherry red with a light tan-coloured convertible top, and it shone magnificently under the autumn sun.

The windows were down and Gracie and I stepped onto the running board, barely resisting the urge to hop inside. I could almost feel what it would be like to sit in the driver's seat, hands on the steering wheel, while the engine rumbled under the hood. Pa had let me sit with him and help steer the truck lots of times, but I knew that wouldn't compare to being behind the wheel in this beauty.

"Just what do you think you're doing?" a man's voice boomed behind us.

Gracie and I whirled around and jumped off the running board to find ourselves facing a man in a dark grey suit and fedora of the same colour. He looked angry.

"Nothing," Gracie said. "Just looking at your car."

"What about you, kid?" he turned his dark eyes to me. "What've you got to say for yourself?"

"We didn't touch anything," I stammered.

"You weren't making to steal my car now, were you, kid?"

"No way!"

"You sure about that?" A smile played at the corner of his mouth. He tucked it away quick, but not before I'd seen it. "After all, it's a pretty nice car. Used to belong to a guy who knew Gary Cooper."

"No kidding, mister?" By then I knew he'd been teasing us, pretending to be angry. "Would I kid you, kid?" He laughed at this and then reached into his pocket and pulled out a key. My heart began pounding furiously for the second time in the space of a few minutes.

"Anyone want to go for a drive?"

"I know I do." Raedine had appeared on the front step. She was leaning against the post, smiling. I was glad to see that she seemed fully recovered from her illness earlier. Her face had a pink glow and she looked very young and happy.

"Can we go in the rumble seat?" Gracie asked, jumping up and down and clapping her hands.

"Unless you plan to drive, I reckon that's the only place left for you to sit," Mr. Manby told her.

As we drove, Mr. Manby told us that the car was a 1938 Packard Super Eight Convertible Coupe and that he'd won it in a card game in Chicago one dark night. Raedine told him not to be talking nonsense and filling our heads with stories about gangsters when the truth was he'd bought it from a used car lot in Regina.

Conversation trailed off after that since we were picking up speed. With the motor revving and the air rushing around us in our seat outside the back of the car, we wouldn't have been able to hear them even if they shouted.

We had half a dozen drives in that Packard over the next month or so, until Mr. Manby quit coming to see Raedine, but none compared to the exhilaration of that first one.

After Mr. Manby there were several other men who visited Raedine. Each of them would come around for a few weeks or even months, but the friendships never lasted much past that.

As winter's snow and wind arrived and filled our fields, this mini-parade of men walked in and out of Gracie's life. They joked around with her, brought her little presents, and called her things like "kiddo" and "squirt." Sometimes it was hard to tell them apart.

There was one who was pretty memorable though. His name was Charlie Lipton and he had black hair that never moved, no matter how windy it was outside. Raedine said that Charlie was rich enough for ten men and, whether or not that was true, he sure seemed to spread money around. He gave Gracie a whole dollar every time he came over and he bought things like dresses and necklaces for Raedine.

One morning, Gracie met me at the bus stop with the thrilling news that Charlie was going to marry her mother and then he'd be her new daddy and no one would be able to say she didn't have a father anymore.

Raedine was like something lit up for a while after that. She talked a lot about the rock Charlie was going to buy for her. That puzzled me until I realized she meant a diamond ring. And she told us that Charlie didn't want her to work anymore after they got married, and it sure didn't sound like she minded the idea of leaving her job.

But Charlie never did produce the rock Raedine was expecting. Instead, just like the others, he stopped coming around. It was a while before Raedine seemed to understand that he was gone for good. When she did, she said things like she sure could pick 'em and she was through with "fellahs" because none of them were any good anyway.

But it wasn't long before she changed her mind. She told us that when you fall off a horse, you have to pick yourself up and dust yourself off and get back out there.

Of course, it would have been impossible for Raedine's men friends to call on her without all of Junction hearing about them. Around the middle of winter the town had decided it was time to show its disapproval once again.

By that time most of the boys my age had completely lost interest in ignoring me. It didn't much matter to me, for I'd come to realize that Gracie was worth a whole heap more than any other friend I had—more than all of the others combined, in fact.

And that was a good thing, because I was still the only friend Gracie had.

I don't know if I fully realized at that point that I loved her. I was barely twelve and I'd never given a full moment's thought to love.

The Glory Wind

But I know it now. And I can tell you that if I live to be a hundred years old, I'll never love another human being more than I loved Gracie Moor.

Valerie Sherrard

PART FOUR

The Sounding

Some of the damages that are blamed on tornados are actually caused by downbursts, or "plough winds." Like tornados, downbursts occur during severe thunderstorms, when powerful concentrations of air plunge to the earth's surface and spread out.

Downbursts have been known to produce straight wind speeds of up to 200 kilometres an hour and can cause a "roaring" noise that is very similar to the sound a tornado makes.

Chapter Nineteen

The way Gracie told it, three callers from the Junction Ladies Circle burst into her house like a winter blizzard on the first Friday evening in March. Gracie did a fine imitation of Mrs. Anderson batting her eyelashes while she said how *terribly* sorry they were for not coming sooner, while Mrs. Stafford and Mrs. Anstruther smiled and nodded.

"What did they want?" I asked, though it was hard to stop laughing with Gracie's face shoved toward me and her eyelashes fluttering like moths at a flame.

"It seemed like they wanted to be friends, but that was only at the start. They all smiled a good deal and everyone admired what Momma had done with the house. Then they talked about how nice it was to see the spring coming and such. I was there for that part, and then Mrs. Anstruther stood up and said there was a matter they'd like to bring to

The Glory Wind

Momma's attention without little ears around."

I had no trouble imagining the mayor's wife making this announcement.

"So then Momma winked at me and told me that was a very secret code which I could probably never understand, but it meant I should play somewhere else so these ladies could speak to her privately." Gracie paused. She looked very solemn.

"*Of course* I wasn't going to miss whatever was coming next, so I went out the front door, around the house, and in the back. I hid under the kitchen table and I heard everything. They started out nice again, telling Momma they were concerned about her and it was their duty to help her."

Gracie took a deep breath. Her eyes were pools of sadness as she continued.

"Then the ladies said Momma was on a dangerous path and that her soul was in *grave danger*. They said they had a prayer team just for Momma the week before, and they believed it was their duty to help her. Then Momma said they could all just help themselves out the door and she left them sitting there and came into the kitchen."

I laughed, picturing the shocked and angry faces of the three women. I stopped when I saw the look on Gracie's small, serious face.

"That's when Mrs. Stafford told Momma she was very, very sorry for her and that they had done their duty to save her soul. And Mrs. Anstruther said *again* that Momma's soul was in *grave danger*, and she feared it may already be too late for Momma to repent."

Gracie's voice dropped to a trembling whisper as she asked, "Do you think it's true, the things they said, Luke? Do you think something terrible is going to happen to my momma?"

At this, Gracie broke down and cried. She cried so hard that she couldn't catch her breath, and all the while her eyes were pleading with me to say something to make it all right. Except, I didn't have the first clue what to say, and I knew she could see that.

"I have to go talk to Carmella!" she said when she could speak again.

Selfishly, my first thought was that the snow was still several feet deep in spite of the early spring thaw we were experiencing. If we went to Carmella's place we'd have to take the long way around, which meant trudging for miles through muck and slush along the roads.

Of course, there was nowhere else to go when there was

something we needed to ask an adult. Through the summer and fall we'd spent many afternoons in Carmella's kitchen, drinking tea or buttermilk and eating biscuits while she answered our questions and told us stories of her childhood. But when winter had arrived in full force, the shortcuts through the fields disappeared and the visits were put on hold.

"Those ladies probably don't even know what they're talking about," I told Gracie, hoping to avoid the long, messy walk.

But she was determined, and when Gracie was determined there was no sense in wasting your time trying to change her mind. She told me she'd go without me if it was too much trouble, and I told her of course I would go and I hadn't meant anything by it, and she forgave me right on the spot, which was a relief. Gracie always forgives me when I've done something wrong, but sometimes it takes a little while.

So, we set off for Carmella's place to ask for answers neither of us could have ever hoped to get at home.

It was cold and windy, but as luck would have it, we didn't have to walk far at all. We'd barely turned the corner onto the road that would take us to the Tait farm when a Plymouth sedan pulled onto the shoulder ahead of us. I recognized it as

Roy Hilbert's car, which surprised me. I'd seen him sitting in church with his widowed mother most Sundays and he'd never once struck me as the friendly or obliging type.

"Need a lift?" he asked as we reached the car.

"We're going to the Tait farm," I told him. Looking down at our feet I thought to add, "Our boots are pretty muddy."

"No matter." He nodded toward the door and we climbed in. The motor went from a rumble to a roar as he pulled back onto the road.

"How are your folks, Luke?" Roy asked as we bounced along over the dips and bumps in the road, which were worse in the spring than at any other time of year.

I told him they were fine and he said I should tell them hello for him.

"And how's your mother, Gracie?" This question was so unexpected that I turned to look at him, but Roy seemed to be concentrating hard on watching the road, even though it ran straight as an arrow for miles and miles.

Gracie told him her mother was fine too, and then he said she should tell her mother he said hello.

"Yes, sir," Gracie said.

"Mayhaps there are times your mother needs something done around the house…something that calls for a man,"

Roy said then. His face was darkening into a near plum shade and I noticed that he was gripping the wheel tightly with both hands. "You tell your mother that I'd be happy to oblige if she needs help at any time."

"Yes, sir," Gracie said. She looked pleased.

"Tell your mother I'd be proud to help out, as a good neighbour," Roy finished up, expelling a breath of relief. I figured that had probably been the longest speech he'd ever made.

By then we'd reached the lane leading to the Taits' house. As Roy pulled the car to a stop, Gracie spoke.

"I think there might be something my mother needs help with," she said, looking right straight at Roy.

It flustered him for a moment but he nodded. "Tell your mother I'll come by tomorrow afternoon. Just to take a look, mind you. I can't actually do anything 'til later on, seein' as it's the Lord's Day tomorrow."

Gracie told him that she'd let Raedine know he was coming, thank you very much, and then we headed down the lane leading to Carmella's house.

"What does your ma need done?" I asked her.

"Oh, lots of things," Gracie said. "She said just the other day that she wishes she had someone around so she wouldn't have to fight with stuck windows and such."

It was a mystery to me why she'd tell him to come over just to shove up some stuck windows. I was still puzzling this through when we got to Carmella's kitchen door. We banged good and hard.

Carmella's cheerful face appeared and she ushered us in, declaring that we were a sight for sore eyes. "Sit right down, sit right down," she told us, bustling about. "I'll put on the kettle and make you some tea with honey to warm your bones after that long walk."

We told her we'd gotten a drive, but she said the lane was long anyway and just kept on with what she was doing. When the kettle didn't boil fast enough to suit her she added a chunk of hardwood to the stove, even though the firebox was more than half full of crackling, snapping wood and flames.

"Now!" she said, once she'd put steaming, enamel-coated cups in front of us and produced a plate of buttered bread. "What brings you two here on a day like this?"

"Some ladies came to see my mother," Gracie said, reaching for a slice of bread. "They said they were there to help her, but the things they said didn't seem one bit helpful." You had to admire the way Gracie could just come right out and say whatever she wanted to, no matter how difficult the subject might be.

"Is that so?" Carmella didn't sound surprised. "What kind of things did they say, honey?"

"They said that my momma's soul was in danger and they had done what they could to help her but it could be too late!"

"Well, they were wrong to say such a thing. And anyway, there's no call for the ladies of Junction to be concerning themselves with your momma's business," Carmella said.

"But they *are* concerning themselves," Gracie pointed out. "And I don't know what it all means, exactly, but it frightened me."

"That's why we came here," I said. "So you could explain it all for us."

Carmella's shoulders slumped a little and her head dropped forward so that her chin rested on her ample chest. She mumbled something that sounded like a prayer and then sat without moving for a full minute or two. Gracie and I sat silently, waiting.

"I declare!" Carmella said, bringing her face up so suddenly that I started in my chair, "you two do know how to put a body on the spot."

Chapter Twenty

"I have a story to tell you," Carmella said after a long pause.

We leaned forward, setting aside our bread and tea in order to give her our full attention.

"Back when my granddaddy was a young man, he worked for a rich man on a ranch in Wyoming. My granddaddy's job was to take care of the horses—brush them down and tend to their shoes and feed them—all the things that have to be done to keep them in fine health.

"Now, one year there was a beautiful chestnut foal born and the white man's daughter loved that foal, so she asked her father if she could have it for her very own. And because he was rich and he loved his daughter, it was in that man's power to give that horse to his child.

"My granddaddy took good care of that foal and it grew into a beautiful young filly and the man's daughter loved it.

The Glory Wind

She wouldn't ride any other horse in the stable no matter what. Now, that horse knew she was special and it showed in the proud way she pranced around or shook her head. And everything was fine for about three years."

Carmella adjusted herself in her seat and took a drink of her tea before going on.

"This horse wasn't meant to be bred or worked, of course. It was just for the daughter to ride. But one day, my granddaddy was terrible sick with a fever, and that fever made him a mite delirious and he put the filly in the wrong field, and in that field there was a stallion. And the next thing you knew, this filly had a foal in her belly."

Gracie clapped her hands at that, which made me and Carmella look over at her. A strange feeling of dread crept into me as I took in the glow of Gracie's face, shining with delight.

"A new baby horse!" she cried. "The girl must have been so excited!"

"Well, now, you might think that. I guess lots of folks would be, but this girl wasn't. She didn't want that horse to change, not one little bit. But the horse was changing, and so, she stopped riding it, and she stopped taking apples and sugar cubes to it. Where she used to spend hours talking to that filly and brushing it, she hardly even looked at it anymore."

"That's awful!" Gracie said.

"Yes it is, child," Carmella agreed. "Well, before long, the girl decided she wanted a different horse and she picked a new foal for herself. Then her first filly—well, I guess she was a mare by then—was put to work to increase their stable by producing a foal every year. My granddaddy declared that that horse had some of the most beautiful foals he ever did see. But it was a changed animal."

"Changed how?" I asked.

"My granddaddy said that horse lost all its joy. She never pranced or held her head up the way she had before, and he said you could see a sadness in the horse's eyes that would break your heart."

"Because the girl didn't love it anymore," Gracie said.

"That's exactly why. But you need to remember that there's a happy side to this story too. Even though it all began because of a mistake, those beautiful foals would never have been born, and the world would have lost them and all their offspring too. And I think that's the most important part of the whole story."

As we were thinking about that, Carmella poured more

hot tea into our cups and slid the remaining bread slices in front of us. "Best eat up and be on your way, now," she said. "It's a cold day and you have a long walk ahead of you."

We did as she suggested and it wasn't until we were halfway home that it occurred to us Carmella hadn't answered Gracie's question at all.

"Maybe she did, though," I said. "Maybe it was like a parable or something."

"What's that?" Gracie wanted to know.

"We learn about them in Sunday School," I explained. "It's a story about one thing that's supposed to teach you about something else."

"Like what?"

"Like, there's one that I heard a few times about this shepherd who had a whole bunch of sheep—I forget how many, but a lot. And one day one of the sheep got trapped on a rock on a hill or something and the shepherd went out in the storm to look for it because he cared about that one little lost sheep just as much as he cared about all the rest of them that were safe."

"Did the shepherd find it?" Gracie asked.

"Yes, because he wouldn't stop looking until he did."

"That's a nice story," Gracie said.

"Yeah, but like I said, it means something else."

"Like what?"

I thought hard, trying to remember it right. "Something about how God cares about lost people and keeps trying to get them to come to Him where it's safe."

"Oh." Gracie nodded. "So you think Carmella's story was one of those pear-apple things too?"

"Parable," I corrected. "I think it might have been. Only, we probably have to be older to figure out what the story was really supposed to mean."

Gracie sighed. "Well, I wish I understood more things right *now*. My head gets so confused sometimes that I feel dizzy."

To demonstrate, she began to weave and spin, flopping her arms out at her sides as she pirouetted along the roadside. It was okay until she tripped on a clump of mud and landed on her hands and knees in the muck and slush.

"Luke!" she yelled, as if I'd made her fall. I knew I hadn't but that didn't keep me from being nervous.

"What?"

"Why didn't you try to catch me?"

I'm almost certain that it had happened too fast for me to react—one second she was whirling and the next she was flying toward the ground. It's unlikely that I had a chance to do anything more than watch.

That doesn't change the fact that I'm haunted by that moment, frozen in time. I can see her face, turned to me, those small brows knitted together in puzzlement. I can feel the hurt behind her words, the inability to understand why she'd felt no movement behind her. If I had lunged forward or reached for her, it wouldn't have mattered that it was too late. She would have known that I'd made the effort.

But I didn't, and her question still troubles me.

Not: why didn't you catch me? But, why didn't you *try* to catch me?

Chapter Twenty-One

"Luke! Luke!"

"Now what on earth is that child on about?" Ma asked, looking up from the shirt she was making for Pa's birthday.

"I dunno." Through the window I could see Gracie racing toward the door, her hair flying out behind her in the April sun. Excitement lit up her face as she called my name again. I hurried to the door and pulled it open as she rounded the corner of the house and came barrelling toward me.

"You'll never guess what's happened!" she said, bursting into the room.

"Hello, Gracie."

"Oh, uh, hello Mrs. Haliwell." Gracie turned back to me after answering my ma's greeting. "Well, what do you think, Luke, but Miss Prutko is getting *married* and moving all the way to Halifax with her husband. That's in Nova Scotia—*way* far away on the other side of the country."

"Oh, yeah?" I tried to sound enthusiastic since Gracie was so excited, but it wasn't easy. I was actually pretty disgusted that the big exciting news was something as dumb as a wedding.

"And *I'm* going to be her flower girl!" As this last bit of news burst out of her Gracie clapped her hands and jumped up and down.

The needle in my mother's hand stopped in mid-stitch and her head came up. "Gracie!" she said with a huge smile. "That's wonderful."

The next thing I knew there was a boring old discussion going on between Gracie and Ma about a dress. It seemed that Miss Prutko was going to see about borrowing one somewhere, but then Ma said she would make Gracie a dress.

When I think about it, my parents don't seem to play a very large role in many of my memories. Aside from a few stand-out moments, they appear very much as shadows in the background. Maybe it was because they were busy most of the time, or because our everyday routine was so unremarkable. Whatever the reason, that's the way it is.

But the smile I saw on my mother's face when Gracie made her announcement, and the work she put into that dress over the next few weeks—these are things I will never forget.

So, Gracie had her dress for Miss Prutko's wedding—not something borrowed and ill-fitting, but a brand new gown, pale pink with a white ribbon around the waist. She looked like a faerie princess in it, with her hair floating free around her face, and her hands dipping into that basket and gracefully scattering flower petals on the bride's path to her new future.

Not that I was there, but I saw enough demonstrations to cover a hundred weddings, and I bore it easily because I could see the happiness shining right out of Gracie. That was something I didn't mind looking at for hours on end.

Then the wedding was over and Miss Prutko was going away, but not before she had a second surprise for Gracie. This one I saw happen for myself because Gracie and I were gathering Hawk's Beard and chamomile for a wildflower bouquet she was making for Raedine. We were engrossed in our task when a car horn honked and drew our attention to the road.

The Glory Wind

"Miss Prutko!" Gracie squealed and then corrected herself with, "Oh, no! I mean *Mrs. Knowling*!"

I followed her as she hurried from the field's edge to the side of the car.

"Hello, Gracie, Luke," our former teacher greeted. "We've just stopped at your house, Gracie, but there was no one home. We left something on the front porch for you—just a little present to remember me by."

"What is it?" Gracie asked, but Mrs. Knowling shook her head and laughed.

"Why don't we take them to see it?" asked Mr. Knowling. He reached over and touched his new bride's arm and gave her a sappy smile. So we jumped into the back seat and Mr. Knowling drove the short distance back to Gracie's house. There on the porch was the painted desk and chair.

Gracie said, "Oh!" and clapped her hand over her mouth. Then she stood up and leaned forward to put her arms around Mrs. Knowling. And she started to cry.

"Oh, dear," said Mrs. Knowling. "Maybe we best get out and sit on the porch and have a bit of a visit before we go, Eddie."

"Sure," said Mr. Knowling. He looked like he'd agree to pretty much anything she said.

We all got out and sat on the porch, and Gracie asked, did anyone care for a refreshment. Both Knowlings said no thank you, they'd just eaten a huge lunch and couldn't manage a single thing. I was about to say I could manage something all right, but Gracie plunked down and started talking about the wedding and the desk, so that seemed to be the end of the offer.

Mrs. Knowling explained to us about how she'd taken the desk back home because she knew they wouldn't let Gracie sit in it anymore after they fired her from her job.

"They *fired* you?" Gracie and I echoed.

"Yes. What did they tell you?"

"That mean old Mrs. Drillon said you quit," I said.

"Oh. Well, I guess I should have known they wouldn't admit to what they'd done," she said quietly. "But the truth is, when I wouldn't do what they wanted, they decided I was no longer fit to teach. It broke my heart to leave that classroom, but I had to stand up for what I believed."

"It broke *our* hearts too—right, Luke?"

"Uh, sure," I said, a bit embarrassed claiming something like that. I'd felt bad when Miss Prutko left but I was pretty sure it hadn't broken my heart.

"Oh, oh!" Gracie said, jumping to her feet. "I bet she

knows, Luke!"

"Knows what?"

"Remember, the girl at the town meeting? She said something happened to her cousin but we could never ask anyone what it was because we weren't supposed to be listening. But I bet Miss Prutko—I mean Mrs. Knowling—knows all about it."

I'd forgotten about that but my curiosity was piqued as soon as she mentioned it. It seemed our teacher's was too, because she insisted we tell her exactly what we were talking about.

I explained how we'd gone with my parents that night and weren't supposed to go near the building but had snuck over and listened at the window anyway.

Mrs. Knowling didn't look very happy about that. She said something about how we should have obeyed, but then she wanted to know what we'd heard.

Between us, Gracie and I gave her as many details as we could remember of the different people who had gotten up and spoken, and how they'd wanted her to take that desk away from Gracie.

"Except for Leah," I said.

"Leah Zecchino?"

"Right. She was talking about her cousin...I forget her name but she had something wrong with her mouth, I guess."

"Eliza. Yes, I remember her," Mrs. Knowling said.

"Well, Leah said something about a tragedy, only she didn't say what it was, and we couldn't ask anyone because then they'd know we were listening to the meeting!" Gracie said. "So, do you know what the tragedy was?"

"It was a long time ago," Mrs. Knowling said, nodding. She paused and took a deep breath. Her face had gone sad and I almost wished we hadn't brought it up, except now I was really keen to find out.

"It was at the end of the summer—oh, I suppose it must be fifteen years ago or more—just a few days before school was to go back in after the holidays. Eliza was a few years younger than me; I believe she was going into grade five or six that year, and I was starting grade eight.

"She'd been picked on a good deal in school. Not by everyone, mind you, but by enough that it must have felt that way to her. And I imagine, looking back, that she just decided she couldn't take another year of it, because just before Labour Day weekend, she tried to do herself harm."

"What did she do?" Gracie asked, her eyes wide and

almost frightened.

"She threw herself down a well." Mrs. Knowling shuddered, remembering. "It was just by the grace of God that her older brother saw her and was able to lower the bucket and climb down the rope in time to save her. She was banged up quite badly but otherwise unharmed. But she never spoke again—not a single word—at least, not as long as the family was still living here. They moved away some time ago and I imagine they keep in touch with family members, but no one ever seems to mention Eliza."

Mr Knowling moved the conversation to lighter things then and after a while they left, hugging both of us good-bye and telling us to write now and then.

I know that Gracie wrote several times over the next months, but I wasn't much for letter-writing and never did get around to it.

Chapter Twenty-Two

I used to wonder where Raedine's men friends came from. None of them were from Junction and, to my knowledge, none of them had any particular business in Junction. They just seemed to show up out of nowhere, come around for a while, and then disappear.

It took a while before that came to an end, though Gracie had put the wheels in motion the day Roy Hilbert drove us to Carmella Tait's place. Roy showed up at Raedine's door the next day, as promised, only Gracie had forgotten to tell her mother about her conversation with him, so it was a total surprise.

Gracie described the way Roy's face had turned purple while he stood there and squeezed his hat and stammered and stuttered a few jumbled words about house repairs to Raedine.

"Momma just stared and stared at him," she laughed. "I

think she had him figured for some crazy person and she was trying to work it out in her mind whether or not he might be dangerous. I had to rescue him by explaining it all to Momma."

"Then what happened?"

"Then she made him tea and told him she was right proud to know him and she sure did appreciate his offer. And he said he'd be happy—*more* than happy—to come by every so often to see if she needed anything done and in the meantime did we have a phone to call him in case of an emergency. And when he found out we didn't, he wrote down his address for her to send him a note if there was anything urgent, and she told him again she was proud to know him, and then he stopped squeezing his hat and put it back on his head and left."

I laughed along with Gracie but I couldn't help thinking that what she'd just described—how poor Roy had gotten all flustered and all—sounded an awful lot like the exact way I felt around her sometimes.

It didn't matter that I was a whole eight months older than Gracie and a year ahead in school; there were lots of times when I felt really small and dumb beside her. I started to ask Pa about that one time, but I only got half of the words out when he had to go check on something that had fallen over in the barn and when he came back the urge had left me.

Well, Roy started to come around Raedine's place pretty much every Saturday afternoon and sometimes one of her boyfriends would be around. Gracie always gave me all the details. One time that was the end of the boyfriend right then and there. He put his jacket on and said something strange about someone else cutting his grass and huffed out the door.

We kept expecting Roy to give up and stop coming around, but he never did. He'd fix anything Raedine asked him to and then sit down and have a cup of tea while the boyfriend of the moment glowered or put on a big show of not caring, or did whatever it was he was going to do. And when Roy had finished his tea he'd leave, but not before he made a point of telling Raedine he'd be back soon.

And by and by, Raedine stopped inviting boyfriends over and she started inviting Roy to stay and eat dinner with them on Saturday night.

Gracie seemed happy about it all.

"I think Roy is going to be my new daddy," she told me one day, and it wasn't two weeks later that Raedine came into my house to pick up Gracie after work and told us all that she was engaged to be married to Roy Hilbert.

"Well, congratulations. That's real nice," Ma said, polite but cool, as she'd been ever since learning that Raedine had lied about her past.

"I'd be honoured if you'd stand up with me," Raedine said. "I don't know many people around here, and you and your husband have been very kind to me."

Ma pressed her lips together. Then she tried to put her polite smile back on but her face wasn't cooperating. She couldn't seem to squeeze any words out.

"Well, you just think it over and let me know," Raedine said. If she noticed that Ma was acting a bit odd, she didn't let on. She told Gracie to come on and they headed home.

The date for Raedine's wedding was set for August 14.

That night when I was supposed to be in bed, but was really listening at the top of the stairs, Ma talked it over with Pa and decided to reconcile herself to doing her Christian duty, even though she didn't have to like it.

Ma said at least she had the comfort of knowing that it was going to be a quiet affair, since Raedine had planned a private ceremony at her house. Besides Raedine and Roy, there would be Pastor Lockhart and his wife, Roy's mother, plus his sister and her husband, who was his best man, Ma and Pa, and Gracie and me.

For a while, it looked like there might be a problem. Roy's mother came to see Raedine and told her she wasn't going to miss her only son's wedding, but she wished she hadn't lived to see the day that he married someone like Raedine. Then Raedine told her maybe she *would* miss her only son's wedding because maybe she wouldn't be welcome, which led to a big fight with Raedine and Roy. Gracie said it was awful the way they yelled at each other, with Raedine telling Roy he had better think hard about who he was going to be married to, and Roy telling Raedine that a man might have more than one wife in his lifetime but he only had one mother.

In the end, Roy brought his mother to see Raedine again, and his mother said she was willing to let bygones be bygones for her son's sake and Raedine said she hoped they could be on good terms someday, and things were smoothed over for the time being.

Gracie brought over the dress my ma had made for her when she was the flower girl at Miss Prutko's wedding. She asked if Ma could let the hem down to allow for the growth spurt she'd had since she'd last worn it. Ma said she most certainly could, and of course Gracie squealed and hugged her.

Gracie was always hugging someone. Of course she hugged her mother a lot, but she also hugged my mother and Carmella and Miss Prutko/Mrs. Knowling. Sometimes Raedine told her to give Roy a hug, and she would, but there was a shyness about him that kept it from being a real hug. And then there was me. Everybody knows that boys don't go around hugging people, but there'd been a few times when I'd had no choice. Gracie could get really, really excited about a thing, and when she did she'd come flying at you and just throw herself around you. I never quite got to the place where I felt *enthused* about it, but after the shock of the first few times I found I didn't mind it too much, providing there was no one else around.

And that was the problem on the morning of the wedding. Gracie had come to our house to ask did my mother have any silk stockings because Raedine had dropped one of hers on the stove while she was rushing about, and of course she had to have silk stockings for her wedding!

Ma had none, but she remembered that Mrs. Guthrie had told her she'd received three pairs from her son on her birthday just a few months ago, and maybe she'd be willing to let Raedine have one.

Gracie thanked her and started toward the door, but she turned just before she reached it. Her face was shiny and flushed and her eyes were lit up.

She said, "Can you believe it, Luke?"

And then she came at me, crossing the room like a charging ram, nearly knocking me backwards, and she threw her arms around me.

"Can you *believe* I'm getting a new daddy today?"

My reaction wasn't deliberate. It was automatic—the reaction of a nearly-thirteen-year-old boy who has just had a girl hug him in front of his mother.

I shoved her away. And I said, "DON'T!"

Gracie stepped back, all the joy draining from her face. I saw her lip quiver. I saw tears start to fill her eyes. She turned and ran out the door.

It all happened so fast that by the time I fully realized what I'd done, she was already racing across the field and away from our house.

Chapter Twenty-Three

I started out the door, meaning to call Gracie back, to tell her I was sorry and that I hadn't meant it when I'd yelled "don't" and pushed her away. Ma stopped me.

"Let her go for now, Luke," she said. "You'll see her at the wedding and she'll have had time to cool off by then."

I should have gone right then and there anyway, but part of me wasn't eager to face up to what I'd just done. If I'd been braver or stronger, then the day may have ended differently. I talked myself into thinking Ma was right, even though my gut told me that she was dead wrong.

As it was, the longest I could manage to sit still and do nothing was about half an hour. My heart was ripping at me at the thought of Gracie's eyes filling up that way and I couldn't shake the image of her face—full of joy and excitement one second and crumbling the next. I couldn't stand the thought that I had brought about that change, especially on a day when she was so happy.

I said nothing to Ma about where I was going in case she tried to talk me out of it again, and slipped out the door, unobserved, the first chance I got. I figured Gracie would have had time to get to Guthrie's house by then, and I was hoping to intercept her on her way back home. I sure didn't want to have to go to her house and face her in front of her mother.

Scanning the horizon, I saw that the dark clouds that had been gathering earlier seemed to be breaking up and floating off in the strong breeze. The sun peeked through here and there and it looked as though it might, after all, be a nice day.

I hit the road running, my stomach tight with the feeling you get when you're about to try to fix something you've done wrong. As my feet pounded along through the dust, all I could think was that I had to make her listen, no matter how stubborn she wanted to be—this time I wasn't going to shrug and stomp off, the way I might if we'd squabbled under normal circumstances.

The only thing I wanted to do was give Gracie back her day. And so, when I saw her, walking through the field, heading back toward her house, I felt my heart lift with the feeling that it was going to be all right.

Gracie would forgive me. Of course she would. There was no other possibility on a day like this.

I scrambled through the ditch and up onto the fence that ran the length of the road and called, "Gracie!" as loud and long as I could. Her little figure stiffened the way you do when you've heard something and are straining to make it out.

"Gracie!" I called again, this time forming a cone around my mouth with my hands. Then I raised my right arm in a slow wave to draw her attention.

She rotated toward me, stopping when she saw my arm. For a moment she stood completely still.

"Gracie!" I yelled again, "I have to tell you something."

I could see, by the way she tilted her head, that she hadn't caught the words. It was hopeless, with the wind so brisk. I stretched up as tall as I could and beckoned her toward me.

She began to move and I felt my insides relax in relief when I saw that she was coming in my direction.

Gracie was wearing a blue and white gingham dress— one I'd seen many times before. I know her hair was tied in pigtails but I can't remember whether the ribbons were blue or white. They would have been one or the other—her hair ribbons always matched her clothes.

I watched her moving through the field, not hurrying, just coming steadily along. She was still almost the full width of the field away when I saw it, a cone shape forming, reaching down from the clouds.

My brain struggled to take it in while the cone swirled and twirled, narrowing more and more at the bottom and sliding down and forward as it spun with ever-increasing speed. Within a moment or two it was as though a cloud snake had slithered from the centre of the cone and begun to reach closer and closer to earth.

Horror gripped me as I realized I had just watched a tornado form. My heart thumped in mad alarm as I watched it head right toward Guthrie's field.

I yelled like a maniac, waving my arms, screaming for Gracie to run to the ditch and get down. There was nowhere she could find shelter in the open field, and no other possible place she might have time to get to. I remembered my pa drilling it into me that the ditch was the best place to go if you were out in the open.

I can't say what she heard or understood of my frantic yells and gestures. All I know is that she stopped coming toward me, turned to look behind her and then froze in place.

I leapt from the fence and tried to run toward her but my movements were slow and difficult as I battled the terrible power of the wind. The air was filling with twigs and leaves but I held my head up so as not to lose sight of Gracie.

I saw her head tilt upward. Oddly, I saw her arms rise, as though she was about to conduct an orchestra. The skirt of her dress lifted and flapped madly around her.

I screamed again, this time calling for her to lie down but it was too late. The spiralling cloud was descending those last few feet, touching the earth only yards away from where Gracie stood. And then it was on her and I could see nothing but the grey of spinning debris and cloud tearing round and round, spitting out plant and earth as it moved.

I fell to my knees, shocked and trembling as the horror began to penetrate. My eyes were fixed on the tornado, straining for a glimpse of blue and white gingham. I had no idea how long it would take to pass over the spot where Gracie had been standing, and I was terrified that she would be badly hurt when it was gone.

I can't recall being afraid for myself, even though the

whirling cloud was moving steadily toward me. It seemed to bend and sway in a dance-like motion for a few moments and then several things happened at once. The whole sky darkened and rain began to pour down in torrents, drenching the ground and pelting hard against my skin. And, at the same time, the tornado seemed to stand still, as though it was pausing, deciding what to do next. Suddenly, it darted to the right, tore a bush from the ground, whipping it off to one side, and then it began to lift.

It hovered in the air, bits of foliage and dirt still flying into the air around it. I watched as it began to spread, its edges becoming less and less distinct. Spellbound, I saw it break up and dissipate until nothing was left but a vaguely v-shaped protrusion from the clouds and even this was barely visible through the pounding rain.

I made my way through the downpour, calling Gracie's name over and over. I stumbled to where I had last seen her and then turned around and around, searching desperately.

There was no sign of Gracie Moor.

Chapter Twenty-Four

I don't know how long Raedine had been there when I caught sight of her. She was soaked, except for her hair, over which she was clutching a plastic rain bonnet.

I watched as she crossed the road and came through the ditch and past the line of trees that ran along the edge of Guthrie's field. I forced my feet to move in her direction. The strangest feeling came over me, as though I was moving in slow motion. Even so, it seemed I was getting close to her far faster than I wanted to.

"Luke?" Her face was very white. I knew she must have seen the tornado but the trees would have prevented her from seeing where it touched down.

I opened my mouth to tell her, but all that came out was, "Yes'm?"

"Luke, did Gracie come to your house a while ago?" There was an edge to her voice, like it was stretched thin and about to snap.

"Yes'm. But my ma didn't have any silk stockings." I could hardly believe my ears. It was as though I had no control over my mouth, and instead of saying the words that were screaming around inside my head, a robot was answering Raedine's questions.

"Where did Gracie go when she left your house?"

"She went to Guthrie's place, to ask about the stockings," I said. The fact that Raedine was dressed in a long pink housecoat registered irrelevantly in my brain.

She sagged with visible relief. "She's there now?" she asked.

"No, ma'am," I said. "She was on her way home when it happened."

"When the...tornado came?" she said weakly.

"Yes'm. And now I can't find her."

Raedine trembled, reached forward into the air, and collapsed. You'd have thought she was made of paper, the way she folded and crumbled to her knees. A horrible cry tore from somewhere deep inside of her.

Whatever force had pressed her down, an opposing one seemed to take hold of her just as suddenly. Her head jerked up and she jolted back to her feet, looking at me with wild eyes.

"Exactly *where* was she the last time you saw her?"

I pointed toward the spot where Gracie had been standing when the tornado swept over her. I didn't tell her I had checked that exact spot just a moment before.

Raedine grabbed my arm and yanked me along as she began to run in the direction I'd pointed. It was all I could do to keep up with her. My feet barely touched the ground as I was pulled along. The wet flaps of her housecoat billowed in the air just ahead of me, all but blocking my vision.

"Here!" I cried as we reached the place where the tornado had touched down.

"Here?" she asked as she reached the spot. She twirled around, looking about frantically. "Are you *sure*?"

I nodded. It was quite obvious from the tornado's path along the ground, where it had begun.

"Then she's here *somewhere*." Raedine said wildly. "We just have to *find* her."

She began scurrying about, her housecoat snagging on the weeds and shrubs in the field. There was no design to her movements; she ran about in all directions, darting crazily, like a chased rabbit. At the same time, she called

Gracie's name, drawing it out in a terrible, lonesome sound. It rose into the wind and rain and was swept off in a ghostly trail.

I suppose I should have been looking and calling too, but I found myself rooted to the spot, replaying the moment the tornado had touched down, trying to find a gap in the scene my brain had captured. I knew I hadn't taken my eyes off the tornado from the time it touched down to the time it wore itself out and broke up, but I hadn't had so much as a glimpse of Gracie after it had reached her.

I strained to remember if something had blown across my field of vision, obscuring the tornado for the tiniest fraction of time, but there was nothing. Even the rain hadn't blocked my vision enough to have prevented me from seeing Gracie being thrown out of the whirling column. And yet, I had seen nothing.

I was still examining these thoughts and images when a movement to the west caught my attention. Shielding my eyes, I saw Mr. Guthrie crossing the field toward us, moving at a country sprint. An enormous sense of relief came over me that I was no longer alone with Raedine— her only source of help.

"Is someone hurt?" he called as soon as he was close

enough to be heard.

"My Gracie!" Raedine gasped out. Her hands clenched into white balls as she gulped for air. "She's missing."

Mr. Guthrie said nothing more until he reached us. "Was she here when the tornado came through?" he asked. Raedine's face gave him his answer.

"Please!" she cried, "Please help me find my baby!" She stepped forward and took hold of Mr. Guthrie's shirt. Her face was turned up to him, white and pleading.

"Of course we'll help you find her," he said, taking her hands and gently moving them away. "Luke, you run home and tell your pa to get help and come quick, your ma too. Miz Moor, you go on over to my house and tell Joan to call for everyone hereabouts that has a phone. We'll cover this farm in no time and find your little one all right. She's probably just stunned and scared, or she may have a broken bone or two and can't move. But don't you worry none— we'll find her, of that you can be sure."

I turned and raced toward .my house, scanning the ground as I went. Mr. Guthrie's words had offered such relief that I felt as though I was scarcely heavier than the air. My feet flew and it seemed that, but for the need to propel myself forward, they may not have touched the ground at all.

Ma was in the kitchen, her head bent over a small package she was wrapping in a pale gold paper. She glanced up when I rushed in, and her face froze in alarm.

"What is it?" she asked. Her hand drifted up to her chest and grasped at a button on her blouse.

I told her, breathless, pushing the words out in a rush, mixing them up and having to go back several times.

Ma was on her feet before I'd finished. Scissors clattered to the floor.

"Your father—he's still in the back field," she said. "Go! Tell him what's happened. Be as quick as you can."

I ran out the door, barely registering the fact that the rain had all but stopped, and started across our fields as she'd instructed, but something had changed. My legs, lithe and powerful just moments ago, had gone weak and rubbery. They wobbled forward, barely holding me upright. I felt sure I would pitch onto my face any moment and yet they somehow delivered me past the barn and halfway through the first field where I met Pa on his way back to the house.

"Your ma send you to fetch me?" he asked with a smile. "I knew she thought I'd forget about having to go to Raedine's wedding, but here I am. You can vouch for me when we get back."

I struggled to arrange the words he'd said into something that made sense. The wedding seemed like something from another time and place. I shook my head.

"The tornado," I told him. "It took Gracie."

He stared hard at me. "What are you saying, son?"

"She was there—in Guthrie's field, when it came through. And now we can't find her."

His mouth twisted and the line of his jaw grew taut but he said nothing. Instead, he reached for me, and, a second later, I felt myself slung over his shoulder. I felt the pulsing strength and power of his body underneath me and I was reassured. Even with his bad leg, it felt as though we made it to the house in no time.

Chapter Twenty-Five

It was amazing how quickly people arrived at Guthrie's field. A few neighbours came hurrying through the fields but most people came in cars and trucks. They pulled up along the roadside and people spilled out of them and made their way to the centre of the field. Everything revolved around the spot where the tornado had touched down—the last place Gracie had stood.

By and by Sheriff Latch and Mayor Anstruther came, each of them looking official and solemn. Sheriff Latch said that he would bring the full weight of his office to bear on the situation and Mayor Anstruther said that he would personally see to it that no stone was left unturned until little Stacy was found.

Raedine marched over and hollered right in his face that her child was called *Gracie* and how was she supposed to feel good about help that was coming from people who didn't even know her name?

The mayor said that he was terribly sorry and it was all so distressing to everyone and they must try to keep clear heads in the face of it, but after he made the same mistake a little while later he just started referring to Gracie as "the precious child."

The full weight of Sheriff Latch's office turned out to be his brother-in-law, Deputy Oscroft, and a couple of cousins that he referred to as his "deputized posse." They went out to walk the fields just like everyone else was doing while Sheriff Latch wrote things on a clipboard he was carrying. I heard him tell the mayor several times not to worry, that he would be sending in a full report, but the mayor just looked annoyed and barely grunted in reply.

There was a great feeling of community, of hope and brotherhood there that day. I lost track of how many people told Raedine not to worry, that Gracie would be found before she knew it. Lines of searchers spread out, walking twenty or thirty feet apart, crossing fields in all directions. Gracie's name was called out over and over until it seemed like some sort of endless echo.

Roy Hilbert was one of the last to show up, but that was because he'd been out of town. Raedine had sent him on errands to pick up some last minute things for the wedding. He pulled up in Raedine's driveway and then crossed the road into Guthrie's field looking as puzzled as you'd expect a man to be who'd come to be married and found his bride in her housecoat in a field with people scattered everywhere around her.

He asked what was going on and Sheriff Latch took him aside and talked to him in a low voice with his hand resting on Roy's shoulder.

"She's not dead!" Raedine yelled when she saw that. "You don't need to be acting that way!"

"No ma'am," Sheriff Latch said, "I just thought you might not want to go over the whole thing again."

Roy shrugged Sheriff Latch off and made his way to Raedine, where he put his arm around her and told her everything was going to be all right. Raedine pressed her face against his chest and began to cry. She started off with tiny choking sobs but they quickly built up to great shuddering wails. Roy kept patting her back and telling her it was going to be all right and once she took a huge breath and looked right up in his face and asked him if he promised.

He pulled her against him and murmured something

The Glory Wind

and patted her hair, and I got so scared that I thought maybe my legs were going to take over on their own and run me right out of there. But I stayed and kept answering the same questions I'd been answering since it happened. After a while it felt as if someone else was talking and I was watching from nearby.

The thing that kept me from disgracing myself and crying like Raedine was the optimism in the air. I'd heard plenty of people say that it was just a matter of finding her and no doubt she was banged up but there was every reason to hope it wouldn't be anything too serious.

The wind died down early in the afternoon, right around the time that Raedine and Roy were supposed to be getting married. The searchers rejoiced and told each other that the calm was a good thing because it would be easier to hear Gracie if she was lying somewhere injured, calling out for help. I heard it repeated in the crowd, back and forth, and everyone smiled and nodded and said any minute now something was bound to turn up.

Then, as though saying it had made it happen, a great shout of excitement came racing across the fields, passing from group to group until it reached us. A child's shoe had been found in a field across the road, near a stand of bur oaks.

Raedine was like a woman possessed when the news reached her. She pushed herself away from Roy and started running like a maniac, screaming, "Gracie!" over and over. Her housecoat flapped madly behind her, exposing her legs as she ran. I found myself staring at them, bare and white, carrying her toward the shoe and hope.

Watching those legs slice along through the field, I told myself that they were to blame! If Raedine hadn't wanted those stupid stockings, Gracie wouldn't have been in that field at all. She'd have been safe and snug in her house, getting ready for the wedding.

She wouldn't have been in my kitchen that morning and she wouldn't have hugged me and I wouldn't have shoved her. I worked hard at trying to make myself believe that it was Raedine's fault, even though I knew the truth.

I wished I had something to hit, right then. Something big and solid that I could pound on as long and as hard as I wanted to. Instead, I clenched my teeth and made low growling sounds that I hoped no one nearby could hear.

I don't quite know why I didn't follow the trail of people that was making its way to the shoe; I just didn't. I stood there in the same earth-torn spot where I'd been most of the day and waited. Sometimes, as crazy as it sounds, I looked straight up, as though Gracie might fall out of the sky any second.

I saw it in the slump of their shoulders as they started to come back and I knew the shoe hadn't been Gracie's. As it turned out, the shoe belonged to Mrs. Guthrie's granddaughter. It had been carried off by their dog months earlier and no one had been able to find it. I heard Mrs. Guthrie tell Mrs. Peascod that it was a shame they'd finally given up and thrown out its mate, now that the missing one was found.

Roy was practically carrying Raedine when they came back. She looked like a rag doll, sagging against him, dragging her feet. I felt sorry for hating her a few moments earlier.

By late afternoon the mood had changed. For one thing, no one was saying anything very encouraging. There wasn't much conversation at all by then but the faces said plenty, the way they were tight and grim and anxious.

And scared. I could feel the fear in the air and I knew it was bigger than my own fear.

Their fear seemed strange to me. I couldn't grasp why they would suddenly care about Gracie, a little girl who they'd shamed and hated and done out of a desk.

Still, they kept on, long past the crawling shadows of evening. It wasn't until the dark made it impossible to continue that they moved off toward their cars and homes. A few tried to tell Raedine not to give up hope but most just said they'd be back at dawn before they faded into the night. I don't think Raedine heard much by then anyway. She'd gone more and more limp as the hours went by, rousing herself only to rage or howl and then sinking back into some private inner place.

Ma took hold of my hand when she started for home and when I tried to pull away, she turned fierce eyes on me, and I dropped the silent objection and let her lead me through the field and along the road to our house.

Chapter Twenty-Six

The search went on for nine days. Dry wind and scorching sun watched over the effort, which swelled and spread and then shrank back in on itself when most of the area was combed for a second time.

I travelled around after the first day, wandering from one search group to another. I listened and watched and it wasn't much into the second day before I gathered that a lot of folk figured I was mixed up about what I'd seen.

I'd hear things like, "If that tornado broke up near here, the way the Haliwell kid said it did—why, we'd have found her long before now. Only possible explanation is that she was carried farther off."

That notion wasn't put to rest until several others stepped up and said they'd seen the same thing. Then there were ideas about wells and trees and other places that the tornado might have dropped Gracie—places where she wouldn't easily be discovered. The problem with that was that everyone hereabouts was looking for Gracie, and everyone knew their own property like the back of their hand, so all of those spots had been carefully explored and ruled out.

I heard folks say that the long, dry stretch of weather we'd just had was a blessing in disguise, hard as it had been on the crops. Aside from the splash of rain we'd had the day Gracie disappeared, the summer had been drier than a burnt boot. The usual little streams and ponds roundabouts were dried up or close to it, and there's not a lake or river within four or five miles in any direction. That helped ease the worry that Gracie had landed in water and drowned.

As the days went by, the searchers talked more and more about other things until Gracie was hardly mentioned much at all. I heard about the crops and livestock and upcoming events and bits of news that had nothing to do with anything that mattered to me.

If Raedine happened nearby the searchers would stop talking and move forward very quietly, choosing their steps with care and sweeping their eyes back and forth over the fields in guilty silence. Sometimes she would say something about Gracie, or about how she appreciated what they were all doing, and everyone would freeze still, like they were playing Simon Says, and not budge until she'd finished speaking and moved on. Hardly anyone ever said anything back.

Raedine stopped in front of me one day and looked right in my face for a long minute like she wasn't quite sure who I was. Then she stepped forward and squatted down and asked me what Gracie looked like the last sight I'd had of her.

"She had on a blue-and-white dress," I said.

"I know what she was wearing," Raedine said. "I want to know how she *looked*! Do you think she was...scared?"

Then, before I could even answer, she stood up quickly and covered her mouth with her hand and walked away. I went and found her later on.

"I don't think Gracie was scared," I told her. "She kind of looked surprised, and maybe curious. And then she turned around and put her arms up like this." I swung my own up to demonstrate how Gracie had looked, from behind, very much like a tiny conductor.

It seemed like a long time before Raedine said anything, and then she put her hand on my head and told me I was a good boy and a good friend to Gracie. That made her start to cry again and she went off looking for Roy, although I think that was the day he had to go and take his mother to the doctor.

There were fewer people coming to help in the search by the fourth day. The farms couldn't be left to tend themselves, so most of the men went back to what they usually did and the women came to help look for Gracie.

Sometimes someone would try to send me on an errand. Old Mr. Downey couldn't search on account of his knees, so he'd been helping out by driving a truck around with water and sandwiches for the searchers. Now and then someone would ask me to go fetch him. That was the thing they wanted most of the time, though there were a few other errands as well.

I never did what they asked. I'd just wander away like I was going to do it and then I'd go off to another field, or I'd cross over to my own property and make my way to the Circle of Truth and I'd lie there and close my eyes and wonder about things.

I can't describe what went on inside me while the search was still happening. Most of the time it felt like there was a pain pushing in on me, and no matter how hard I tried to push back, it kept closing in tighter and tighter.

I was scared, there's no doubt about that. But I wasn't always sure exactly what it was I was scared of. Obviously I was worried about Gracie, and I knew pretty early on that chances were she was hurt bad or worse. I didn't want anything bad to have happened to her, but I knew what I wanted wasn't going to make any difference to anything.

Maybe that was it. Maybe it was the kind of fear you get when you realize that what you want doesn't matter. You can want something so bad that every cell in your body just aches for it, but it doesn't change things one lick.

I couldn't stop going over and over the last day, and the way I'd acted. I kept trying to remember it differently, and trying to make myself believe that it wasn't my fault that Gracie had been in that exact spot when the tornado came.

And I spent a lot of time thinking about Gracie and me and all the things we'd done and talked about. I tried hard not to cry, but sometimes it seemed to happen on its own, and I hated that because it was girly and it made my chest hurt something terrible.

And then, sometimes my attention would slip onto something that had nothing to do with Gracie. If they'd been big, important things, it might not have seemed so bad, but it wasn't like that. They were always small things, and meaningless, like an oddly shaped leaf or some unusual bug scurrying along in the sand or a glistening fleck in a stone. It would take me the longest time to pull my attention away once some unimportant object had captured it.

The hours and days stretched out until all the trudging through fields seemed as if it would never end. But mostly, the search began to seem pointless. The hope that had been so strong early on had thinned and faded until I couldn't even find its shadow. I knew that was true of everyone else too—I knew it because I watched them as they moved through the fields, their eyes sweeping back and forth as they went. There'd been a change. They'd gone from searching to just looking, and even that was in an automatic way that said they didn't expect to find anything.

Raedine was around less and less. Someone said the doctor had given her "something to help," and that she was making liberal use of it and sleeping a lot. I didn't know how it could help for her to sleep when she could have been out looking like everyone else, but no one else seemed to find that odd.

When she did come to the fields, you could feel the tension right away. It hadn't been that way the first few days—when hope was still there. Now, Raedine's presence just made the searchers uncomfortable. I guess they were all thinking that it wouldn't be long before they were lining up to tell her they were sorry for her loss.

The Glory Wind

They talked about calling it off on the seventh day. The searchers had gathered in Guthrie's field, as they did at the end of each day, as dark was falling. There, they talked about any progress they'd made or anything unusual they'd seen, and they made plans for the next day before they all headed wearily toward their homes.

"We've covered a lot of square miles and done it twice now," Sheriff Latch said, though he'd personally covered nothing. He just drove around and wrote things on his clipboard. You could usually find him wherever the food and water truck was. "I don't know if there's any point in us keeping on."

No one agreed with him, but no one disagreed either, which was just about the same thing as agreeing, under the circumstances.

"Fact is, there's just nothing else we can do. Much as we'd all like to see this thing resolved, we're out of options."

"You going to tell that to her mother?"

Like everyone else, I turned to see who'd asked that. A strange sensation went through me to see that it was Leah Zecchino. Most everybody looked away quick, but a blush ran through the crowd and I knew they were remembering her words at the town meeting.

"On the other hand, it wouldn't hurt to keep on for another day or two," Sheriff Latch said as though he'd just thought of it. "But I can't be neglecting the duties of my office any longer, so I won't be here full time. I'll stop by, mind you, but just now and then. In the meantime, if anything happens, get to the nearest telephone and call me."

There were no calls to Sheriff Latch over the next two days. Fewer searchers showed up on the eighth day, fewer again on the ninth, and when that had come and gone with no results, it was clear that even the last hangers-on weren't coming back.

"They're going to stop searching," Ma said, standing at Raedine's door with a tin plate of cabbage rolls later on.

"Stop?" Raedine repeated, like it was a new word to her.

"There's nothing more that can be done," Ma said. "We've looked everywhere and looked again. I'm afraid it's in God's hands now."

Raedine stared at her silently.

"Roy isn't here?" Ma asked when it was clear Raedine wasn't going to speak. I wondered why she needed to ask, since his car was nowhere to be seen.

"His mother is ill," Raedine said. Then she closed the door and left my ma standing there holding the cabbage rolls.

PART FIVE

The Aftermath

The greatest danger from a tornado isn't the wind itself—it's flying debris. Chunks of glass, wood, brick, and countless other materials can become deadly missiles in a tornado's high wind, leaving behind enormous damages to repair and clean up.

Chapter Twenty-Seven

How it all turned into something other than a missing girl named Gracie Moor, I never did figure out. One day everyone was out in the fields searching for her, calling her name, giving each other hope with words and looks, and then all of a sudden it was different.

The first sign I had that something was shifting came at church the third Sunday after Gracie disappeared. Or, rather, I should say *after* church. I suppose that's an important distinction.

Pastor Lockhart had preached about sowing and reaping, though I can't say I paid a great deal of attention to the sermon. I had the vague idea that he was talking about the crops, sort of a theme message like at Christmas and Easter, only for harvest season. But that wasn't it at all, apparently.

The Glory Wind

We filed out in the usual way after the closing hymn, with everyone shaking the pastor's hand and most of the adults complimenting him on the sermon. Then, there was always a bit of after-service chatting—inside if the weather was bad and outside when it was fine.

This day being sunny and warm, folks stood around outside, talking idly, making plans for later in the week and discussing the little things that filled their lives.

I was hungry as usual after church and anxious to get home, change into everyday clothes, and have a steaming bowl of leftover borsch which my mother had made the day before. To distract myself from the pangs in my stomach, I moved around, ignoring the other kids and eavesdropping on what was being said in the little clusters of people.

I'd learned long ago that listening in on adults' conversations wasn't hard just as long as they didn't realize that's what you were doing. You could practically stand right beside them and take in every word, provided they thought you were doing something else. It was as simple as looking busy—like maybe poking something with a stick, or holding a stone or leaf and looking hard at it.

That's what I was doing as I meandered in and around the little clusters of people that were gathered, and it was how I first became aware that the sermon hadn't been about the harvest after all.

I hadn't meant to stop and listen to anything Mrs. Brown and Mrs. Melchyn were saying. They're old and mostly talk about their joints and pains and visits to the doctor. But as I passed by them my attention was caught by Mrs. Brown's comment, "It's a pity that Moor woman doesn't darken the doorway here now and again. She might have learned something from this morning's service."

"Truer words were never spoken," Mrs. Melchyn agreed.

Now, *that* struck me as very strange. I'd have thought that the harvest would be the last thing Raedine might care about at any time, least of all weeks after her daughter had disappeared. I decided there was something more to it, something I'd missed. Getting as close as I could without looking suspicious, I bent down to examine some imaginary thing in the dirt.

"I hear that no one has even seen the woman for almost a week, maybe two. She hasn't left the house or answered her door in days, and her curtains are all drawn," said Mrs. Brown.

"I suppose she's having a difficult time of it, with the child's body not yet found. I think that would be the worst—not knowing for sure what happened to her," answered Mrs. Melchyn.

"A judgment," Mrs. Brown said, with a solemn shake of her head. "That's what's happened."

There was a pause then and I sensed one of them glancing at me, realizing someone was nearby. I ran my finger through a small mound of sand and tried to look intrigued.

"I suppose you're right," Mrs. Melchyn said.

"No supposing to it!" Mrs. Brown's voice hit a higher pitch. "It's all black and white, you know. Right there in the Good Book."

"I've never read anything about a tornado snatching away a child," Mrs. Melchyn sniffed. "And you don't need to talk to me like I'm a simpleton."

Mrs. Brown tried to sound contrite. "I'm only saying that it's just like the pastor pointed out this morning—Raedine Moor reaped what she sowed."

"I didn't hear the pastor mention Raedine Moor. Not once."

"Well, of course he didn't. He's not going to start naming names. That wouldn't be Christian. But it's clearly what he meant."

The conversation was interrupted just then by Mrs. Melchyn's son, who came to tell her they were ready to go. I moved along but found myself unable to concentrate on anything else I heard that morning.

At home, setting the table while Ma stirred the pot of borsch heating on the stove, I decided to ask about it.

"Was Pastor Lockhart talking about Gracie's mom this morning?"

"Raedine? Of course not, Luke. Where did you hear such a thing?"

"I heard someone say something like that when I was walking around," I said vaguely.

"Well, it's just not so," Ma told me. She stopped making slow circles in the pot with the big wooden spoon and came to the table, nodding for me to sit down. "Were you paying attention to the message?"

"I thought it was about the harvest," I answered. No need to mention that I hadn't exactly focused on what Pastor Lockhart was saying.

Ma smiled. "In a way, it was. Only not so much about harvesting crops, as deeds."

"Deeds?" I'm sure I looked as puzzled as I felt.

"Mmm, for example, if you're mean to someone and

then one day you want to borrow something from that person, what do you think will happen?"

"They won't give it to you?"

"They might not," she agreed. "Everything we do brings about results in just the same way. Some you can see and figure out quite easily, and others are harder to see and difficult to understand. But our actions are a lot like planting seeds—they all grow into something—even if it's just the kind of person we are."

"So, how does that have anything to do with Raedine?" I asked, unsatisfied with how the conversation had gone. It felt like one of those talks we had when I asked a question Ma didn't really want to answer.

"What exactly did you hear about Raedine?" Ma asked.

"Something about the tornado taking Gracie because Raedine sowed or reaped or something."

Ma was silent for too long and when she answered, it was slow and deliberate, and I could see she was being careful about picking her words. Whenever she did that it reminded me of how I step when I'm walking along on something narrow and it feels like I might lose my balance and fall off any second.

"It's not our place to judge other people," Ma said.

Her failure to out-and-out contradict what Mrs. Brown had been saying weighed heavily on me as I tried to sort it all out. I knew that if Ma thought what Mrs. Brown said was wrong, she'd have told me so. Since she didn't do that, I figured that she at least thought it was possible Mrs. Brown was right.

That was when I began listening to local talk in earnest. Only, now it wasn't a game, something to do to amuse myself and maybe pick up interesting bits of news. Now it seemed there might be some kind of answer out there— something that would explain what happened to Gracie.

I think part of me wanted to believe that Raedine was somehow to blame for everything. If she was, then I might be able to rid myself of the horrible guilt I was carrying. What had happened the day Gracie disappeared was never completely out of my thoughts.

I made up my mind to find the truth. And I decided to start at the one place where I could ask a question outright and expect an answer.

The very next morning, I set out to visit Carmella Tait.

Chapter Twenty-Eight

Carmella was outside, hanging clothes from a big wicker basket when I came in sight of her place. I could tell when she saw me because she stepped away from the laundry and stood there waiting. Normally, she'd have hollered my name out, but this time she just stood there—still and unsmiling.

"Luke. How you doing, honey?" she asked when I'd nearly reached her.

"Okay, I guess."

She nodded, like I'd said a lot more than that and she was agreeing with all of it.

"Come on. We'll go in and have a cup of tea," she said. "I'll finish up here later on." She reached a hand out and put it on my shoulder as we walked toward the back door.

"I've been wonderin' when you'd be finding your way here," she said. "I reckon you have some things you need to talk about."

Of course, I'd seen Carmella over the previous weeks. She'd joined in the search effort like most Junction residents, and she'd been in church as usual every Sunday. But there'd never been a chance to really talk to her.

"I've been hearing things," I said once Carmella had spread butter on some thick slices of oatmeal brown bread for us, poured the tea, and seated herself across from me. I don't think Carmella hardly knows *how* to talk without a cup of tea in front of her.

She nodded, giving me time to sort out what I wanted to say and how I wanted to say it. That was another thing I liked about her—she didn't rush me or jump in and try to guess what I was going say. Some folks do that and all it does is make you feel like you're taking up too much of their time.

I started out slow, telling her about the conversation I'd overheard on Sunday morning.

"What does it all mean?" I asked when I'd finished.

Carmella pressed her lips together and shook her head. She took a deep breath, let it out and then looked upward, as though there might be something written on the ceiling that would help her.

The Glory Wind

"Luke, you know I don't like to speak out against anything your mamma has told you—or at least failed to contradict. But in this case, I've got to. I can't sit still and listen to these things and stay silent."

In spite of that, it was a full minute or two before she spoke again. "It's wrong, just plain wrong for folks to be talking like that about that little child—like she was some kind of punishment for the way her mamma lived her life. Now, I'm not saying that Miz Moor was doing right, but to say the Good Lord poured down His wrath on that little child…it just don't sit right in my heart.

"Now you know I love the Lord, and I try to live my life by what He shows us in the Good Book. I don't judge others, no sir, and I don't mean to be startin' now. But I feel a righteous anger in me toward anyone who says that precious child was took up for those reasons. Because I do believe, and I will believe this to my dying day—that what happened to Gracie Moor was a miracle."

"A *miracle*?" I repeated, astonished. That was about the last thing I was expecting Carmella to say.

"A miracle! That's what I said. Just like Elijah, when he got lifted up to glory without ever passing through the valley of the shadow of death. That's what I believe in my heart happened to Gracie. The Lord just took her up into heaven."

"How come?" I asked.

"How come? We don't get to know those things, child! Not this side of glory anyway."

I thought about that for a bit, while Carmella hummed a hymn between sips of tea and bites of brown bread.

"Does anyone else think what happened to Gracie was a miracle?" I ventured after a bit.

"I hear some things that make me think so. Mind you, no one came here discussing it," she said. "It's just a shame that folks are saying those other things. That's how the old devil takes away the blessing—by putting ideas into people's heads and making them think wrong about something the Good Lord did for His purpose.

"If you stop to think about it, you can see that it stands to reason. It's been weeks now since that wind reached down from glory and took our little Gracie. If something else happened, why, they'd have found something of her by now, even if it was a piece of dress or a lock of hair or something. But they didn't, and that's because she was lifted right on up straight to heaven. That's the only time there's nothing left behind and that's how I know I'm right."

The Glory Wind

Carmella reached across and patted my hand. "I know you miss her, Luke. I sure do too. I knew right from the start there was something special about Gracie. Seemed almost like she was too good for this world. I just don't understand why people have to be so mean, saying what they're saying. It seems they always want to think of the worst thing and believe *that*. And I can't understand why it is."

I felt a little better when I left Carmella's house that day. Even so, it seemed as though something was missing—like I needed a deeper explanation before I could be satisfied.

Chapter Twenty-Nine

I turned thirteen on October 15, 1947. For the first time, I was glad that we had Mr. Wolnoth for a teacher and not Miss Prutko or anyone like her. Miss Prutko had kept track of everyone's date of birth and we always sang "Happy Birthday" after morning prayer and clapped for the birthday boy or girl. We were supposed to do something nice for them too but I don't remember anyone ever actually doing that, unless it was a girl in an older grade latching onto an excuse to make a fool of herself over a boy.

Mr. Wolnoth never started the day with anything special. Each morning, as soon as we'd sung "God Save the King" and said "The Lord's Prayer," he told us, "Be seated, be quiet, and begin working," in the same dreary tone he used every morning.

That suited me just fine. If it had been up to me, my

birthday would have been forgotten altogether, but there was no way that would happen at my house.

Ma had asked me wouldn't I like to have some friends over for some games and cake, but she hadn't pushed it when I said no. I guess she knew that the only friend I would have invited wouldn't be coming.

After we'd eaten supper that night, Ma brought out a cake with candles on it and I dutifully blew them out. Pa pointed out that I was thirteen, like I might not have realized it. Then my folks gave me a copy of *Treasure Island* by Robert Louis Stevenson, wrapped in paper that had footballs all over it. There was also a package with three pairs of woollen socks my grandma had knit for me.

"You'll have to send Grandma a nice thank-you letter," Ma said. I said I would, and I tried to look excited about the book, but it's hard when happy things only make you sadder.

All I could think about was that Gracie and I would have read the book together and acted out the best parts, like we'd done with her book *Tahara, Boy King of the Desert*. Thinking that made me want to throw *Treasure Island* in the stove.

Two months had gone by since Gracie had disappeared

and I was no closer to understanding it than I had been the day it happened. I'd heard two different opinions, but I had no way of knowing which was true. Maybe neither side had it right. Besides that, the hurt—and guilt—never stopped gnawing away at me and it was starting to take its toll.

I put the book in my room and then slipped out the door, wanting to be alone. After wandering aimlessly for a while, I found myself walking along the road toward Raedine's house.

I knew I should have gone to see her before then but I hadn't found the courage to do it. This time, I forced myself to turn in and the next thing I knew, I was knocking at the door.

Raedine opened it just as I was about to give up. When she saw me, she dropped to her knees in one motion and I thought she was going to faint. But she reached her arms out and her face was crumbling as she clasped me against her.

The next thing I knew we were both crying. She held onto me while we sobbed until I was crushed and soggy. It felt as if this was what I should have been doing the whole time. Crying with Raedine. It was the first time I'd felt somehow *content* in months, and I thought (rather oddly) that if only I could stay there and keep on crying, I'd be *happy*.

The Glory Wind

Raedine was the first to get stopped. She mopped me up a bit with the sleeve of her blouse and drew me into the kitchen where she poured me a glass of milk and herself a glass of wine.

"I sure am glad to see you, Luke," she said.

"I'm sorry I didn't come to visit you before."

"Before doesn't matter," she said. "How are you doing?"

"I miss Gracie a lot."

Raedine nodded and took a sip of wine. She set the glass on the counter beside her.

And then, without planning to, I found myself telling Raedine all about that terrible last day—what I'd said to Gracie and what had happened afterward. By the time I got to the end I was crying again, but at the same time I felt like a weight had fallen away from me.

"So, you think it's *your* fault Gracie was in that field?" Raedine said.

I nodded, choking on the hurt in my throat.

"What about me? What if I hadn't needed stockings and I'd never sent her out the door that morning? Or what if your mother had had a pair and she didn't have to go to Guthrie's for them?"

Raedine's hands took hold of my shoulders and she

paused until I looked up at her. Then she went on.

"What if Mrs. Guthrie never had a son, or her son didn't give her stockings for her birthday? Or, how about if Roy's mother never met his father and he was never born so I was never going to marry him? What about all the other things that had to happen beforehand?"

My heart had been beating furiously with the guilt and shame of my confession but it began to slow as Raedine spoke.

"Luke, you've got to believe and understand this. A thousand things—more than a thousand things—all worked together to put Gracie in that exact spot at that exact moment. Unless you can find a way to make yourself responsible for every last one of them, then you've got nothing to feel guilty about."

Relief flooded over me as I saw the truth in Raedine's words. And it was more than what she said that freed me. If she'd shown any sign that she thought it was my fault, well, it would have finished me right then and there, but there was nothing like that.

"I've been trying to figure it all out," I said after a bit.

"You and me both, kid." She reached toward the wine glass but drew her hand away without picking it up.

"Maybe we can put our heads together and come up with something."

I'd carefully rehearsed what I was going to say so as not to make Raedine feel any worse than she already did. But now, it was gone—every word of it. Turns out, I needn't have worried.

"I suppose," she said, "that you've heard all the talk around town. Half of them want to make Gracie into some kind of angel and the other half are busy painting me as the devil himself." She shook her head. "I guess I didn't help that. I've given them lots to talk about, right from the beginning."

"You mean because you weren't married?" I asked. As soon as the words were out of my mouth I realized how impertinent the question was, but Raedine didn't seem offended.

"That was the start of it, all right. It's true I wasn't married to Gracie's father, but that didn't mean I didn't love him. And he loved me—and Gracie!" Raedine said, lifting her chin a little. There was a spark in her eyes but it vanished as quickly as it had appeared.

"He *wanted* to marry me," she continued. "He would have too; he just never got the chance. See, Gracie's father wasn't…free…to marry at the time, but he was going to take care of that, as soon as he came home from the war. Only, he never did come home."

"Gracie always said he was a hero," I said, remembering her announcement the first day we met.

"That was true, Luke. He *did* die a war hero. And you know what? My heart was just as broken when he died fighting overseas as if he had been my husband. But he wasn't." Raedine looked down, until her eyelashes nearly touched her cheeks. Her voice dropped to a whisper. "He was someone else's husband. And she was the one who stood by the casket and the graveside and was surrounded by sympathy and comfort, while I laid on the floor in my tiny apartment and wondered if I could even get my next breath and tried to think of who would take care of Gracie if I couldn't.

"I had to do all my crying and hurting in secret. I was pretty good at keeping secrets by then, but that sorrow was the hardest one to hold onto. It seemed it could just lay me at its mercy any old time it wanted to. I wished I could hide away but I couldn't because I had a child to feed and care for, and that's the only thing that kept me going most days for a long time.

"But by and by, two years had passed and the hurt had gone into a kind of numb ache, and I made up my mind that I was going to get out of there and make a new start and somehow give Gracie the things she didn't have. Like a father. And I may not always have gone about looking in the best ways, but if I harmed anyone, I like to think it was only me. I don't know if God punishes folks for hurting themselves."

"Do you believe in God?" I asked her, somehow surprised that she'd mentioned Him.

"Of course I do. Why, just look at the way the world is put together—everything with its own job and place. I don't pretend to know much about most of those things, but it's always been clear to me that this all had to be designed."

"Do you think God planned what happened to Gracie too?"

Raedine looked up, looked right at me. She sighed. "Well, there sure are plenty of folks around here who believe so. Roy's mother, for instance, and she didn't waste a minute persuading him this was all a judgment against me. He denied it of course, but I could see the fear in his eyes and I knew he would never feel quite the same way about me again. So that was that. I haven't seen hide nor hair of him in more than a month."

She looked so sad and lost that I wished I had something helpful to say, but there were no words in me. It was a relief when she gave her head a little shake and started to talk again.

"You know, Luke, I can't help wondering who these people think they are, going around claiming to know what *God* is up to. How *could* they?

"People have too much pride, if you ask me. They can't stand to say they don't know something—especially when there's a chance to judge someone else.

"The minister and his wife were kind enough to call on me after…what happened, and a few others came by, but then there was no one. I can tell you those days were long—and the nights felt like they had no end."

Her words cut into me, though I know she hadn't meant them to. I thought of the times I'd known I ought to go and see her—and there she was, just aching for someone to talk to, but I hadn't gone. It was tough to shove aside the remorse and swing my attention back to what she was saying.

"I even went to church one Sunday," she continued, "just

wanting to find a little comfort, thinking there might be some kindness there. But all I felt in that building was the excitement of people who thought they might see me fall on my knees and confess or repent or something. I might have known, really, and saved myself the humiliation if I hadn't been so desperate. After all, these are the people who can sit around forgetting everything *they've* ever done wrong in their *own* lives, while they smugly talk about how Gracie disappearing was some kind of punishment God is using to slap me.

"I know I haven't lived the best life I could have, but I'll go to my grave without ever being sorry I had Gracie, so if that's what they were waiting for they'll be waiting a long time."

And then she said it—the thing I'd been waiting to hear. Something my heart could embrace and hold onto as true.

"All these people jabbering on and on, speaking for God, like they know exactly what He meant. Both sides are guilty, as far as I'm concerned, whether they're claiming what happened was a miracle or a punishment. I don't know much about faith, but I do know it's not some kind of guessing game."

I let Raedine's words sink in. She seemed to understand that something important had just happened for me because she stopped talking and just stood there, waiting quietly.

I'd never really given any thought to what faith was before that moment. It seemed an abstract thing, something you couldn't define or touch.

I'd thought faith was what you believe and that was it. But I suddenly saw that believing was only a part of it. After all, belief is something you think—but you can be mistaken in your thoughts. And you can change your mind and stop believing something, so faith must go past that. Faith must be a kind of trust that doesn't need to understand something to know it's so.

It's strange, that the least likely person around opened the door for my heart to find the answer it needed.

EPILOGUE

It's been a year since Gracie disappeared. I think most folk around here expected that something would turn up someday—a bone, a piece of cloth, a clump of that wild curly hair…some scrap to prove that there was once a little girl named Gracie Moor.

Nothing has.

Everyone thought Raedine might leave town—after all, Junction hasn't exactly thrown its arms around her, but she's still here.

I asked her, one afternoon while we were sitting out on her back step eating wild strawberries, why she stays.

"I've got no choice," she said. "When that tornado took my Gracie, it took my options too."

"Do you think there might still be…something… found?"

"You know what, Luke? I really don't. The first months

I waited and hoped for just about any little thing that would make it all final. But I've stopped believing anything will ever be found."

"Then why…?"

"Why can't I leave?" She paused, examining the red berry stains on her fingertips. "I can't leave because I need to see that field when I go out my door every morning. I need to look into Gracie's room and see the bed she slept in and the window she pressed her nose against. I need to be where there are things to remind me that I once had a little girl. I can't take a chance that she'll fade away into a shadow in my mind—until I start wondering if I might have dreamed it all."

I wanted to ask her, that day, if she was very lonely, but the words wouldn't form. I suppose she must be, though she always seems oddly content when I stop by. Maybe she's made up her mind that this is her life and that's all there is to it.

The first months after Gracie was gone I spent a lot of hours in the Circle of Truth. At the start, I'd lie there and swallow down as much as I could to keep from bawling like a girl, but there were times I couldn't help it. Other times I'd close my eyes and pretend Gracie could hear me, and I'd talk to her about anything I wanted to, and tell her how much I missed her.

Now, I like being in the Circle because it reminds me of the things Gracie and I did together—the games we played and the things we talked about. If I close my eyes and lie back and listen hard, sometimes I can almost hear her laughter rippling through the warm summer air.

Also by Valerie Sherrard

PICTURE BOOKS
There's a GOLDFISH in my Shoe
There's a COW Under My Bed

JUVENILE NOVELS
Tumbleweed Skies
The Glory Wind
Watcher
Three Million Acres of Flame
Speechless
Sarah's Legacy
Sam's Light
Kate

SHELBY BELGARDEN MYSTERIES:
Searching for Yesterday
Eyes of a Stalker
Hiding in Plain Sight
Chasing Shadows
In Too Deep
Out of the Ashes